옥화

〈K-픽션〉 시리즈는 한국문학의 젊은 상상력입니다. 최근 발표된 가장 우수하고 흥미로운 작품을 엄선하여 출간하는 〈K-픽션〉은 한국문학의 생생한 현장을 국내외 독자들과 실시간으로 공유하고자 기획되었습니다. 〈바이링궐 에디션 한국 대표 소설〉 시리즈를 통해 검증된 탁월한 번역진이 참여하여 원작의 재미와 품격을 최대한 살린 〈K-픽션〉 시리즈는 매 계절마다 새로운 작품을 선보입니다.

The 〈K-Fiction〉 Series represents the brightest of young imaginative voices in contemporary Korean fiction. This series consists of a wide range of outstanding contemporary Korean short stories that the editorial board of *ASIA* carefully selects each season. These stories are then translated by professional Korean literature translators, all of whom take special care to faithfully convey the pieces' original tones and grace. We hope that, each and every season, these exceptional young Korean voices will delight and challenge all of you, our treasured readers both here and abroad.

옥화
Ok-hwa

금희 | 전승희 옮김
Written by Geum Hee
Translated by Jeon Seung-hee

ASIA
PUBLISHERS

Contents

옥화
Ok-hwa

여자가 떠났다. 아니, 떠났다고 한다.

"언니, 정말이에요. 아까 기차 안이라고 제게 전화 왔더라구요." 정아가 말했다. 오후 나절의 해가 아직 남아 있어서 귀갓길의 그림자가 땅바닥에 길게 드리워 있을 때였다.

"갔으니까, 이제 됐어요 언니. 내일 기도모임 나오시죠?" 정아는 뭔가 칭찬이라도 바랐다는 듯 한참 들까불다가 이내 전화를 끊었다.

'이제 됐어요'라니? 뭐가 됐단 말인가? 얘는 말을 참 이상스레 하네, 하고 홍은 생각한다. 아파트 입구가 가까워온다. 일 층에 사는 리따예가 자기 집앞 돼지기밭에서 궁싯궁싯 걸어나오고 있다. 손에 들린 물조리 뒤로 금방 옮긴 듯

The woman left. No, Hong had heard she'd left.

"Sister, I'm telling you the truth. I got a phone call a while ago. She said she was calling from the train," Jeong-a said.

The lingering afternoon sun was drawing the long shadows of people on their way home.

"Since she left, it's all set now, Sister. You're attending tomorrow's prayer meeting, aren't you?" As she was expecting a word of appreciation from Hong, Jeong-a chatted on for a while before she hung up.

It's all set now? What was all set now? What a strange remark! She drew near to the apartment building entrance. Li Ta-ye from the first floor was

한 오이묘며 토마토묘가 줄느런히 서 있는 것이 보인다.

"그냥 사서 드시지, 허리도 안 좋으시면서……." 그네 앞을 지나치며 홍은 알은체를 하지 않을 수가 없다. "이잉, 밭이라구 있는디 그놈을 걍 놀리믄 워디 쓰겄나? 머라도 심궈 먹어야지." 리따예는 구부정 구푸렸던 허리를 최대한 뒤로 곧게 펴며 벙싯 웃는다. "하여튼 간에, 한시름은 놓았겠네요 이젠." 홍도 웃었다. 모처럼 만에 리따예의 펴진 허리를 보니, 홍 자신도 모르게 같이 허리를 쭉 펴며 숨을 들이마셨다.

겨우 여자가 떠났다는 말에 이리 시름이 놓이다니, 한심한 것. 홍은 금방 들이켰던 숨을 다시 훅 내뱉는다. 그렇다면 여자가 있었던 동안은 정말 짐스럽고 힘들었다는 얘기가 아닌가. 어두컴컴한 계단을 터덕터덕 올라가며 홍은 생각한다. 여자의 툭 불거져 나온 광대뼈와 꺼진 볼살과 찌르는 듯한 눈빛이 다시금 떠오른다. 여자 생각만 하면 마음속 어딘가 찝찝해지고 껄끄러워지는 것은 어쩔 수 없다. 왜? 여자가 불법체류 탈북자라서? 아무것도 가지지 못한 구제대상이라는 것 때문에? 아니면 그 까칠한 표정이며 진위를 가릴 수 없는 변명이 싫어서였을까?

10

walking hesitantly out of the miniature vegetable garden in front of her unit. Hong could see rows of cucumber and tomato seedlings that seemed to have just been transplanted.

"Why don't you just buy them? You should take care of your bad back, you know." Hong couldn't help giving out advice like that, even when just passing by Ta-ye.

"Well, but, when I have this patch, how could I not use it? I have to plant whatever to eat." Li Ta-ye smiled while trying to stand up straight as best as she could.

"Anyway, you don't have to worry any more for a while, do you?" Hong said, also smiling. Looking at Li Ta-ye standing up straight—an unusual scene—Hong also straightened her back unconsciously and took a deep breath.

Hong had felt so relieved just because a single woman had left. How pitiful she was! Hong sighed. So, this meant that she really was bothered and burdened by her while she was here, didn't it? Hong pondered this as she ascended the darkened stairs.

She could remember the woman's high cheek-bones, sunken cheeks, and penetrating eyes. Whenever she thought about this woman, Hong

철컥, 현관문을 연다. 거실바닥 소파 앞에서 마구 뒹굴구는 남편과 아들녀석의 옷가지가 먼저 눈에 들어온다. 그런 이유들이 전부는 아닌 것 같다. 신발을 벗고 들어서기 바쁘게 홍은 맥없이 널부러진 빨랫감을 주섬주섬 주워 모은다. 남편 바지주머니 안에서 뭔가가 만져진다. 꽤 빳빳한 푸른색 종이, 돈이다. 그래. 따지고 보면 이런 것 때문이 아니겠는가?

"미안해요, 점말 미안함네다." 하고 여자가 홍을 불렀었다. 구역에서 수요 기도모임을 마치고 막 나오던 길이었다. 홍은 멈춰서서 그녀 뒤에 약간 처져 따라 나오는 여자를 바라보았다. 올백으로 넘겨 묶은 머리 때문에 여자의 얼굴은 더 길고 눈꼬리는 더 찢어진 듯 보였다. 무슨 말을 하고 싶은 겐가? 여자가 가까이 다가오는 동안 홍은 슬금슬금 불안해했다. 교회에 나온 지는 이년 정도 되었다지만, 이 기도모임에 나온 지는 고작 이개월 남짓밖에 되지 않은 여자를, 홍은 잘 아는 편이 아니었다. 여자는 홍의 반응을 미리 예상이라도 하고 있었다는 듯 생각보다 차분한 어투로 말했다. "이땀에, 내 한국 가믄 절대 갚을 꺼니께, 돈 쫌 꿔주시라요?"

had to admit she felt undeniably confused and uncomfortable. Why? Was it because the woman was an illegal North Korean escapee? Or was it because she owned nothing and needed people's assistance? Or maybe because Hong didn't like her emaciated face and her suspicious excuses? Hong opened the door. What entered her vision first were her husband's and son's clothes thrown here and there in front of the sofa. She thought that the reasons she had just given herself for her discomfort might not be the whole story. As soon as she removed her shoes and entered her apartment, Hong began to collect the dirty clothes article by article from the room. She could feel something in the pocket of her husband's pants. She pulled it out and saw it was fairly stiff blue paper: money. Well, come to think of it, it must have been all because of money.

"I'm sorry. I'm really sorry," the woman had said to Hong on their way out of their Wednesday prayer meeting.

Hong had stopped and looked at the woman who was following her a little behind. Her hair had been bunched up and tied behind her. Her face looked even longer and her eyes even thinner.

빨래를 돌려놓고 홍은 밥솥을 부신다. 싱크대 안에는 마른 밥알이 들러붙은 공기며 반찬을 담았던 그릇이며 찌개를 끓였던 냄비까지 꽉 차 있었다. 가게가 멀어서 매일 아침 일찍 나가야 하는 홍은 아침 설거지를 거의 하지 못하는 편이다. 오늘은 평소보다 먼저 들어온 까닭에 남편의 귀가는 물론 아들녀석의 하교시간도 한참 남았다. 작으나마, 남편과 함께 일궈온 건축자재가게 덕에 중고 아파트도 사고 봉고차도 한 대 장만했다는 말은, 기도모임 중에 홍 자신이 얼결에 뱉었을 것이다.

"돈이요?" 하고 홍이 눈을 크게 뜨며 되묻자, 여자는 기계적인 웃음을 지어 보였다. "모도 다 바빠하는 거 암네다. 기래도 상점 한다니께, 딴 사람들보다는 쫌 안 바빠할 거 같아서요." 어른의 손에 들린 과자봉투를 바라보는 아이처럼 여자는 홍의 얼굴을 빤히 들여다보았다.

"글쎄, 우리도 뭐, 외상장사라 늘 빚에 시달리니까. 우리 아저씨가 뭐랄지……." 홍은 여자의 집요한 눈길을 피하며 두서없이 주절댔다. 왠지 경찰로부터 심문받는 죄수 같다는 느낌이 들었다. 주여, 이런 난처한 일이 내게 오다니요, 어찌하면 좋겠습니까……. 홍은 당장 집 안으로 되돌아가 구들에 엎드려 처음부터 다시 기도

What is it that the woman wanted to tell her? Hong felt uneasy seeing the woman approaching.

Although it had been two years since the woman had begun attending the church, it had only been two months or so since she had started attending prayer meetings. Hong didn't know her very well. As if she had been anticipating how Hong would respond, the woman had said more calmly than Hong expected, "Later, once I get to South Korea, I'll absolutely repay you, so could you please lend me some money?"

After turning on the washing machine, Hong washed the rice pot. The sink was full of rice-encrusted bowls, plates of old side dishes, and earthenware pots. Since Hong had to leave home early every morning because of her long commute, she could rarely do the dishes in the morning. Today, however, she had come home earlier than usual, so it would be awhile until her husband and son would return home. It must have been Hong herself who had said—during their prayer meeting and without thinking—that her family could buy a secondhand apartment unit and a van thanks to the small building supply store that she was helping her husband run.

"Money?" Hong had repeated, her eyes wide.

하고 싶다는 생각이 들었다.

"아니, 머 점말 없다면야, 기래도 거저 한 사천 원이래
도 안되나요? 내 진짜 무신 궁리가 없어서 기래요. 집값
은 석달치 못줬구, 내는 허리가 아파서 일도 못 나가니
께……." 말을 끝낼 즈음에 여자는 홍을 '집사님'이라고
불렀다. (여자는 목사님도 항상 '목사'라고 불렀었다) "쫌 방조
(幇助)해줘요, 집사님……."

'만일 형제나 자매가 헐벗고 일용할 양식이 없는데
(…) 더웁게 하라 배부르게 하라 하며 그 몸에 쓸것을
주지 않으면 무슨 이익이 있으리요.' 야고보서 2장의 구
절이 머릿속에서 필름처럼 지나갔다.

그래서 홍은 그랬다. "사천은 힘들 거 같은데……. 암
튼 주일날 봬요."

사천이나 삼천이나 기왕에 줄 것 같으면 사실 오십보
백보 아닌가. 그런데도 굳이 여자가 원하는 액수에서
얼마만큼이나마 깎아서 주고 싶은 심보는 무엇 때문일
까? 저녁을 먹고 설거지를 마치면서 홍은 내일 있을 기
도모임을 생각한다. 여자가 기도모임에 나오기 전에는,
아니 여자가 돈 얘기를 꺼내기 전에는 한 번도 빠지지

The woman had smiled mechanically and said, "I know everyone's having a hard time. Still, since you have your own store I'm guessing you've been having less of a hard time than others." She stared at Hong's face like a child looking at an adult with a bag of candy.

"Well, we're not really, you know, people buy things on credit, so I don't know what my husband will say, you know…" Hong rambled, avoiding eye contact with the woman. She somehow felt like she was a prisoner being interrogated by the police. Oh, Lord, how can I deal with this kind of awkward situation? What should I do? Hong felt like going back inside, kneeling down, and praying again.

"Well, if you really don't have any money. Still, couldn't you lend me just 4,000 *won*? I really don't have any other options right now. I have a three-month back rent and I can't work because of my back…Please, help me, Madam Deacon." Hong hesitated for a moment. This was a woman who otherwise always referred to their church leaders without the title of "reverend" and the like.

At that moment, words from James 2 went through Hong's mind: "If a brother or sister be naked, and destitute of daily food, and one of you say unto them…be *ye* warmed and filled; notwithstand-

않고 참석하던 모임이다. 가게에서 일꾼들과 점심을 해 먹고 바로 떠나면 시간이 얼추 들어맞아서 남편의 눈치가 덜 보여 딱이었다.

서로를 위로하고 하나님께 의지하는 기도시간도 좋았지만, 기도하기 전 커피 한 잔씩 마시면서 사춘기에 들어선 아들 얘기며 무뚝뚝한 남편 때문에 속상한 얘기와 시집식구 친정식구와 있었던 에피소드를 두루 꺼내놓고 수다 겸 교제하는 시간이 홍은 참 좋았다.

여자가 홍한테 돈 얘기를 꺼낸 뒤, 홍에게는 이상스레 그 기도모임에 가지 못할 사정들이 생겨났다. "집사님, 요즘 많이 바쁘세요? 통 얼굴 볼 새가 없네." 무단결근한 직원 대신 전화통을 붙잡고 스트레스가 쌓여 있는 홍에게 박사모님으로부터 두 번인가 문안전화가 왔다. "그러게요. 생각지도 못한 일들이 자꾸 터지니 계속 빠지게 되네요. 기도해주세요." 아무런 눈치도 못 챈 듯한 박사모님에게는 일단 그 정도로 얘기할 수밖에 없었다.

"언니, 혹시 말이야, 그 북한 자매님, 언니한테도 돈 꿔달라고 얘기했어?" "……." 여자를 보기로 한 주일 하루 이틀 전에 정아에게 연락이 와서야 홍은 피해자, 아니 여자의 '자외선 망'에 걸린 이가 자기만이 아님을 알

ing ye give them not those things which are need-
ful to the body, what *doth it* profit?"

Hong said, "I'm not sure if I can come up with
4,000. But let's talk about it on Sunday."

If she wanted to help her, what difference would
it make if she lent her 4,000 or 3,000 *won*? Why did
she want to give less than the woman wanted?
Dinner had ended and Hong was finishing the
dishes. She thought about tomorrow's prayer
meeting. She had attended it without fail before the
woman had joined—no, before she mentioned
borrowing money from Hong. She could make it
about on time if she left after finishing lunch with
the employees at the store. The timing was good
because she didn't have to leave in the middle of
work and so draw her husband's attention.

Hong enjoyed not only the prayer time, when
they comforted each other and renewed their
commitments to depend on God, but also the time
of socializing when the members of the congrega-
tion would share their difficulties, about adolescent
children and unfeeling husbands, as well as all
kinds of trials having to do with in-laws and families.

After the woman had brought up the subject of

게 되었다. "그지? 그럴 줄 알았어. 그 자매님, 원래 장년
1팀에 있었잖아. 알아보니까 거기서도 몇 천 원 모금했
더라구. 그것두 이번에만. 한 이 년 거기서 신앙생활 했
었다니까, 그전에 찔끔찔끔 도와준 거는 숫자도 없
고…… . 이번엔 한국으로 간다고 교회측에서도 얼마
구제금으로 내놓은 모양이야. 주보에 광고가 나가서 그
자매님 앞으로 들어온 헌금도 있었다나…… . 아 참, 그
리고 박사모님이 제의해서 우리 기도모임 멤버들도 성
의껏 했었는데…… ."

정아는 전화를 끊으면서 그랬다. "언니 말고도 개인적
으로 부탁한 사람들이 또 몇 명 있어. 나한테도 얘기하
더라구. 나는 뭐, 원래 없으니까, 없다고 했어. 차비나
하라고 이백 원 쥐여주고. 그니까 언니도 알아서 해."

가게 사장들이랑 한잔하러 간다는 남편은 늦어지고
있고, 아들녀석은 저녁 먹기 바쁘게 제 방으로 들어가
서 숙제에 열중이다. 남편이 가져다 둔 장부를 펼쳐 들
고 홍은 거실에 있는 책상 앞에 마주 앉는다. 오늘은 배
달이 세 건 있었다. 반품도 두 건 있었다. 물론 수금은
한 계절이 지나가거나 연말이 되어서야 일부분 가능하
다. 수금할 기일이 다가오면 유난히 까탈스러워지고 무

money, though, curiously, a host of "inevitable" circumstances prevented Hong from attending the
prayer meeting from that point on.

"Madam Deacon, are you very busy these days? I
haven't seen you for a while," Mrs. Pak would say in
her calls to Hong, who was sitting, beleaguered
and hassled, in front of a phone, filling in for an
employee who was absent without proper warning.

"My goodness, unexpected things keep popping
up, so I just haven't been able to attend the meetings. Please pray for me," Hong would answer Mrs.
Pak, who didn't seem to know anything about what
had happened with the woman.

"Sister, by any chance, did that sister from North
Korea want to borrow money from you?" Jeong-a
asked her a day or two before Hong was arranging
to meet the woman. That's when Hong realized she
wasn't the only victim to have gotten caught in that
woman's net.

"She asked you, too, didn't she? I knew it. That
sister, you know, she originally belonged to the
Middle Age 1 Team, right? It turned out that she
borrowed a few thousand *won* from them, too. But
that's how much she collected this time only. She
belonged to that team for about two years and
people gave her small sums many times before

례해지고 연락도 쉽게 끊어지곤 하는 가게 사장들이 떠오른다. 생각 같아서는 좀 적게 벌더라도 현금치기 장사를 하고 싶지만, 이 바닥에서 외상은 이미 정해진 룰. 그게 싫으면 그만두는 수밖에 없다.

가게 덕에 먹고는 살지만 유동자금은 항상 딸리는 편이라 여자에게 주려고 마음 먹은 그 돈도 사실 남편 몰래 저축했던 비상금이다. 사천 원이라……. 기약에도 없는 먼 길을 떠나는 이에게 그것이 얼마나 도움이 되겠느냐마는 또한 온갖 수모 당해가며 수금해들인 돈 중에서 한 푼 두 푼 남겨온 홍에게 있어 그것은 땀이고 심혈이었다.

여자를 만나기로 한 주일, 오전예배를 마치고 성가대 가운을 정리하다가 홍은 정아 얘기보다 더 찝찝한 소식을 듣게 되었다. "아니, 집세는 교회서 벌써 대줬다더라구. 재정부 최권사님이 그러던데?" 쏘프라노팀의 팀장 차집사랑 춘자가 그 여자 얘기를 하고 있었던 것이다. "그러게요. 올봄에 나도 보모자리 하나 알아봤줬는데, 뭐 어디가 아프고 저쩌고 말이 많더라구요."

같은 성가대에서 익히 아는 사이들이라 홍이 한 마디

too. And then because she said she was going to South Korea this time, I heard that the church itself also gave her some money. The church even advertised her need in the weekly newspaper and people donated money specifically to her. My goodness. And finally, because Mrs. Pak suggested it, *our* members also helped her as best as we could..."

Hong listened to all of this without saying anything and at the end of the call, Jeong-a stated her final thoughts: "There are a few more people than you whom she's talked to personally. She asked me for money, too. But, you know, I don't have money so I just told her that I didn't have any. I just gave her 200 *won* for her fare. It's up to you how you should handle it."

Hong's husband had gone out for drinks with some of the other storeowners who were also their customers. He wouldn't be coming home and her son was already busy doing homework in his room immediately after dinner. Hong sat with the account book at the desk in the living room. There were three deliveries and two returns today. Bill collection was possible only after the season's or year's end, and only partially at that. When collection time drew nearer, the storeowners became

껴들었다. "몸이 아프면 할 수 없지. 아픈데 어떻게 해?"

정아 또래인 춘자가 그 말에 입을 삐쭉 내밀어 보였다.

"나도 그런 줄 알았죠 뭐. 나중에 보니까 여기저기서 일
자리 알아봐준 사람들이 꽤 있었나보더라구요. 보모는
힘들어, 그냥 밥만 하는 자리는 너무 멀어, 공장일은 위
험해, 어느 회사 청소자리는 시간이 너무 길어……. 아
니 요즘 취직하기가 얼마나 어려운데, 이건 뭐 찬밥 더
운밥 다 가리다 나니. 글쎄요, 여기저기 아프다고는 하
던데 어느 집사님이 사준 쌀주머니는 잘도 메고 가더라
니, 그 말을 어디까지 믿을 수 있겠어요."

들어서 덕이 될 것 하나 없는 얘기들이었지만 어쩌다
보니 물은 이미 엎질러져 있었다. 탈의실을 나서며 차
집사는 춘자랑 눈을 마주쳤다. "뭐, 북에서 온 사람치고
이 자매님이 처음도 아니고, 그전에 있던 사람들도 다
들 말이 많았잖아요?" '전에 있던 사람들'이란 말에 홍은
얼굴이 확 달아올랐다. 차집사는 알고 하는 얘기가 아
니었겠지만, '전에 있던 사람들' 중에는 홍의 남동생과
잠시 인연을 맺었던 여자, 옥화도 포함되기 때문이었다.

오후예배 내내 홍은 머릿속이 복잡했다. 설교 내용이
어느 성경구절인지는 적지도 못했을뿐더러 찬양시간

extraordinarily difficult, impolite, and incommunicative. Although Hong and her husband would have liked to make cash transactions only, credit was the rule in this business. If they didn't like this arrangement, they could quit.

Although Hong's family made a living thanks to their store, they didn't have much liquid money. The money she thought of lending the woman was the emergency fund she had saved behind her husband's back. 4,000 *won*? That wouldn't be of much help to someone on her way to strange, far-away land. But to Hong, who had saved every odd penny from hard collection after collection, amidst every snide remark and open insult, 4,000 *won* was sweat and blood.

On the Sunday Hong was arranging to meet the woman, she overheard even more uncomfortable news while putting the choir gowns in order. Deaconess Cha and Chun-ja were talking about the woman as well.

"Well, I heard that the church has already paid her back rent. I heard that from Madam Choi in the financial department."

"Hmm...I found a nanny position for her this spring, but she said she'd been sick off and on."

에마저 혼자 엉뚱한 장을 펼쳐놓고 앉아 있었다. 교회 화장실에서 손을 씻고 있던 여자를 처음 봤을 때, 홍은 본능적으로 여자의 몸에서 풍기는 북한 냄새를 알아차 렸다. 옥화랑 많이 비슷한 뒷태며 분위기에 홍은 그때 한참 동안 가슴이 벌렁거렸다. 여자가 옥화와는 다른 사람이라는 것, 장년부 1팀에서 이미 일 년간 신앙생활 을 해왔다는 것을 알고 나서도 홍은 가끔씩 여자와 스 쳐지날 때마다 심장이 부르르 끓어오르곤 했었다. 그나 마 여자랑 한 소속이 아니어서 부딪칠 일이 없겠다 싶 어 다행이라 생각했는데…….

자잘한 숫자들이 굴을 파인 개미떼처럼 눈앞에서 오 글거리고 있었다. 머릿속까지 개미떼가 천방지축 오글 오글 기어다니는 것 같다. 장부를 덮으며 홍은 일어선 다. 숙제를 마치고 어미 눈을 피해 컴퓨터 앞에 살짝 들 어앉은 아들녀석을 닦달해서 씻기고 이불 속에 밀어넣 는다. "아침 일찍 일어나야지, 깨울 때마다 더 자고 싶다 고 투정 부리면서." 몸만 컸지 철은 한참 없는 아들녀석 의 엉덩짝을 찰싹 갈겨주고 나서 홍은 방을 나선다.

아직도 들어오지 않은 남편한테 홍은 자신이 모으고 있던 비상금의 존재를 비밀로 하지는 않았다. 그러나

Hong knew them well and so she couldn't help interjecting, "But if she's sick, she can't work, right?"

Chun-ja, who was about Jeong-a's age, pouted. "That's what I thought, too. But then I found out later that many people have found jobs for her. But the nanny job was too hard, the cook position she had to travel too far, the factory job was too dangerous, the company janitor job meant working too long...My goodness! These days when it's hard enough even finding a job she can't be so choosy. I just don't know. She's complained about her back pains, but she obviously carried a bag of rice that a Deaconess bought her with no problem. How much more can you believe her?"

Overhearing them was no help, but it was too late. As she left the changing room, Deaconess Cha exchanged glances with Chun-ja. "Well, Sister Yi wasn't the first North Korean escapee. Other, previous escapees were all trouble, too, you know."

The phrase "previous escapees" made Hong blush. Although Deaconess Cha wouldn't have known it, "previous escapees" included Ok-hwa, a woman with whom Hong's younger brother had enjoyed a brief married life.

All afternoon, Hong was distracted. She not only couldn't write down the correct Bible verses, but

여자에게 준 삼천 원까지 남편한테 일일이 얘기할 수는 없었다. 홍과 함께 옥화를 겪어본 남편은 과연 여자를 믿을 수 있을까? 홍 자신도 무슨 도깨비에 홀린 것 같다는 생각이 드는데.

예배가 끝나고 사람들이 흩어져갈 때에 홍은 문 어귀에서 서성이면서 자신을 기다리고 있는 여자를 보았다. 홍은 짧게 숨을 들이켜며 은행카드가 들어 있는 가방을 집어 안고 자리에서 일어났다. 이왕 도와주기로 한 거, 대답까지 한 거, 해야지…… . 그러나 금방 머릿속에서는 다른 목소리가 들렸다. 아니, 내가 왜? 내가 뭐 빚이라도 졌나? 굳이 줘야 하게? 사천 원이 누구 껌값이야?

사람들이 모두 문 쪽으로 우르르 밀려가서 예배당 안은 잠시 혼란스러웠다. 여자도 밀려나오는 사람들 때문에 하는 수 없이 문 바깥쪽으로 나간 것 같았다. 그때 누군가 홍의 팔꿈치를 쿡 찔렀다. "집사님, 혹시 그 북한 자매님 만나시려고요?" 훤칠한 키에 몸에 맞는 정장을 입은, 지긋한 나이의 기품있는 여인이었다. "아 네, 최권사님." 하고 말하면서 홍은 어느새 그녀에게 끌려 대열에서 빠져나갔다. "물론 이웃을 도우라고 하나님이 그러셨지만, 우리가 모든 사람들 다 도울 수 있는 게 아니

she also sat with the wrong pages of the hymn-book open during the worship service. When Hong had seen the woman wash her hands in the church's bathroom for the first time, she instinctively smelled a particular North Korean scent from her. Her heart palpitated for a while, staring at her back, seeing the aura that reminded her of Ok-hwa. Even after she found out that she was not Ok-hwa, but, in fact, a member of the church and had be-longed to Middle Age 1 Team for a year now, her heart would thump whenever she passed her by. She just thought it was lucky that she didn't have to run into her very often since they didn't belong to the same team.

Tiny numbers were swarming in front of her eyes, like ants spilling out of unearthed tunnels. It felt as if those ants were swarming and crawling inside her brain. Hong closed the account book and stood up. After making her son, who had snuck in front of the computer, after finishing his homework, wash up, she tucked him in.

"You have to get up early," she reminded him. "Whenever I wake you up, you always complain that you want to sleep more," Hong delivered one playful spank to her son's bottom. He was big and yet still so childlike.

니까, 그렇잖아요? 교회 안에도 도와줘야 할 사람들이 너무 많은데……."

홍은 그 말뜻을 금방 알아들을 수 없어서 벙벙하니 서 있었다. 페인트 회사를 운영하는 사장답게 최권사는 언제 봐도 카리스마가 넘쳤다. "내가 뭐 이래라 저래라 하는 게 아니고, 혹시 그 자매님에 대해서 얼마나 알고 있을지 해서요." 사장이라지만 언제 한번 교회 안에서 그걸로 틀을 차려본 적 없고, 절기면 절기, 행사면 행사 때마다 헌금 가장 많이 내고 어려운 성도들 있으면 자기 호주머니 털어서 도와주는 최권사임을 홍은 잘 알고 있었다.

"어제 우리 목회자 운영회에서 그 자매님이랑 얘기했거든요. 이 상황에서 한국으로 떠나려는 게 무리가 아니냐, 여기서 합당한 일을 찾고 마음 맞는 사람 만나 사는 건 왜 안 되느냐고. 참, 여태 그렇게 도와주고 해도 감사하는 마음도 없고, 열심히 해야겠다는 생각도 없고 입만 벌리면 변명에, 돈 달라는 말뿐이니, 쯧쯧." 최권사는 홍을 보며 머리를 저었다.

그리하여 그 여자는 성도로서의 믿음은커녕 인간으로서 기본적인 도덕이나 정직한 양심 따위마저 있는지

Hong's husband hadn't returned home yet. Hong hadn't entirely kept the emergency funds a secret from her husband. Still, she didn't feel she could tell him that she had given 3,000 *won* to the woman. After their experience with Ok-hwa, could her husband trust her? Hong herself was also feeling like she had been possessed by a ghost.

When the worship service had ended and the people had begun to disperse, Hong noticed that the woman was lingering. She was waiting for Hong at the door. Hong took a short breath and scooped up her purse. Her bankcard was inside. She stood up. She had promised to help her. She had to keep her promise.

But why her? Why on earth her? Did she owe anything to those people? Why should she? Was 4,000 *won* nothing?

As people crowded towards the door, the church was in slight disorder. The woman seemed to have gone outside, pushed along by the crowd. Suddenly, someone nudged Hong's elbow.

"Madam Deacon, are you by any chance meeting with that North Korean sister?" It was Exhorter Choi, a tall, graceful, elderly woman in a well-fitted suit.

"Oh, Madam Exhorter Choi," Hong responded

여부가 의심스러운 사람이 되었다. 홍에게 있어서 사실 그 정보는 무슨 새삼스럽거나 받아들이지 못할 만큼 충격적인 것은 아니었다. 그러나 사람들이 거의 빠져나간 뒤 여자랑 만났을 때 머리가 한결 더 복잡해진 것은 사실이었다. 이제 홍의 머릿속은 도저히 실마리를 찾지 못할 정도로 뒤죽박죽이 되어 있었다. 무슨 말을 해야 할지, 뭘 해야 옳은지 아무 결론도 내지 못한 채 홍은 운명에 떠밀리듯이 여자랑 교회 문을 나섰다.

대문 근처 도로변에는 주일이라고 도시 어딘가에서부터 꾸역꾸역 찾아온 거지 서넛이 제법 익숙하게 진을 치고 서 있었다. 그 거지들은 번화가에서 구걸할 때처럼 묵묵히 앉아 있거나 이마를 땅에 박고 절을 하는 것이 아니라, '하나님은 세상 사람을 사랑합니다'라는 참신한 교회식 표현을 신도들에게 날리고 있었다. 다른 날 같으면 일 원짜리 지폐라도 칠 벗겨진 컵 안에 넣어주겠건만 그날은 잔돈도 없었거니와 그럴 마음도 일지 않아서 홍은 무표정한 얼굴 그대로 그들을 지나쳐버렸다. "씨발, 예수쟁이라는 게 동정심도 없어?" 적선 한 푼 없이 지나가는 홍의 등뒤에서 거지들은 언제 처량한 거지 신세였나 싶을 정도로 험한 욕지거리를 질펀하게 퍼

and was led outside of the crowd.

"Of course, God told us to help our neighbors, but we cannot help all people, right? There are so many people that need our help in our church..." Exhorter Choi looked at Hong knowingly.

Not immediately understanding what she was saying, Hong just stood for a moment. Exhorter Choi was charismatic, becoming her position as owner of a paint company.

"I don't mean to tell you what to do, but I wonder just how much you know about that sister," Exhorter Choi said.

Although a company owner, she had never been arrogant in the church. Hong knew how she had always donated the most for celebrations and events and helped poor church members.

"Yesterday, we talked with that sister at the church leader meeting. It seemed unreasonable for her to go to South Korea in her situation. So we asked why she couldn't find a job and man appropriate for her here. But, goodness, she didn't seem grateful for our help so far. She didn't seem to have the will to work hard. All she had was excuses and requests for money. The nerve!" Exhorter Choi shook her head.

And so that woman had become a person with

부어댔다.

여자는 한 손으로 허리를 짚으며 주춤주춤 홍을 따라
갔다. "집사님, 거기 쪼꼼 천천히 가시라유." 공상은행
자동현금지급기가 저만치 보이는 골목에서 여자가 홍
을 불렀다. 홍은 시계를 들여다보았다. 세 시 반이 아슬
아슬하게 넘어가고 있었다. 네 시 전까지는 가게에 들
어가기로 남편이랑 약속이 되어 있는데 허리를 두드리
는 젊은 여자는 저만치서 기신기신 걸어오고 있었다.

"긴데요, 집사님. 점말 미안한데, 당장 바쁜 거 아니머
는 그 돈 쪼꼼 더 해주시면 안 되갔시요?" 허리가 정말
아픈 건지 얼굴을 찡그리고 간신히 홍 앞으로 다가온 여
자가 그 말을 꺼내는 순간, 홍은 은행이고 뭐고 다 집어
치우고 그길로 택시를 잡아 떠나고 싶은 충동을 느꼈다.

불을 끈다. 빛으로 충만하던 공간은 모두 순식간에 몰
려든 어둠으로 전부 대체된다. 묵직하고 끈적한 어둠은
흡사 방 안의 소리까지도 뒤덮은 것 같다. 홍은 자리에
누워 눈을 감는다. 하루가 지나가고 있다. 하루 동안 있
었던 일들도 지나가고 있다. 무엇이든지 간에 모두 지
나가기 마련이고 지나간다는 것은 그리 나쁜 일이 아니

questionable moral beliefs, someone who did not seem to possess an honest conscience, let alone true Christian beliefs. To Hong, all these facts were not necessarily new or shocking. However, it was true that when she met the woman outside after everyone left, she felt considerably more confused. Now Hong's brain felt so completely scrambled that she couldn't tell head from tail. Hong left the church entrance with the woman, not knowing what to say or how to act, as if she was being pushed by fate itself.

Along the street near the church gate, a few homeless people, who had apparently come because it was Sunday, stationed themselves skillfully outside. They didn't just quietly sit or make abject obeisance on the street, like they usually did downtown. Instead, they were exhorting with Christian-style expressions, like "God loves everyone in the world."

On other days, Hong might have put a one-*won* bill into their array of cups. But now she neither had any small bills nor felt like giving them money, so she walked by indifferently.

"Fuck, and you call yourself a Christian? And not even a second look?" The homeless people showered her with curses from behind, suddenly shift-

다. 어쨌든, 여자가 떠났다고 하지 않는가.

그날 밤, 홍은 이미 떠나가버린 여자와의 남은 감정을 끄잡아 안고 또다시 혼자 끙끙거리며 연 며칠 꾸었던 비슷한 꿈속을 헤매고 다녔다. "왜 내가 줘야 하지?" 하고 홍이 묻자 "가졌으니께." 하고 여자가 대답했다. 홍은 자꾸 옥화로 변하려 하는 여자를 붙들고 물었다. "그래서 줬잖아, 근데도 뭐가 불만이야?" 하면 여자는 매번 꿈속에서 볼 때마다 그랬던 것처럼 찢어져 올라간 눈으로 홍을 찌뿌둥하니 내려다보았다. "그 잘난 돈, 개도 안 먹는 돈, 그딴 거 쪼꼼 던재준 거 내 한나도 안 고맙다요."

'그딴 거'라니? 어떻게, 어떻게 그렇게 말할 수가……. 홍은 꿈속에서도 가슴이 답답하여 손으로 박박 내리 쓸어보았다. "내도 한국 가서 돈 많이 벌어봐라. 내는 너들처럼 안 기래." 홍의 몰골을 보고 피식 웃던 여자는 급기야 킬킬대며 배를 부여잡고 웃어대다가 옥화로 변하고 말았다.

사오 년 전, 아직 살아계셨던 엄마가 비밀스럽게 데려온 여자가 있었다. "야야, 후딱 내래온나. 함 바바라, 아

ing from the pathetic vagabonds they'd played a moment ago. The woman had begun hesitatingly following Hong. She said, "Madam Deacon, could you please walk a little more slowly?"

When they reached an alley from which the Gongsang Bank ATM machine was visible, the woman called out to Hong. Hong looked down at her watch: it was a little past 3:30. She had promised her husband she would be at the store by 4. The young woman was walking falteringly quite a few steps behind her, massaging her back as she labored on.

"Well, Madam Deacon. I really am sorry, but if your situation is not too bad right now, would it be possible for you to lend me just a little more money?"

As soon as the woman said this, standing in front of Hong, her face twisted from perhaps real back pains, Hong felt the impulse to ignore her and take a taxi right then and there to the store.

Hong turned off the light. The bright space had been replaced instantaneously and entirely by darkness. The heavy, almost adhesive darkness seemed to cover all the sound in the room. Hong lay down and closed her eyes. The day was pass-

가 참말로 참하다." 흔치 않은 백화점 세일을 만나 명품을 헐값으로 사온 듯한 흥분된 목소리였다. 간만에 톤이 활짝 높아진 엄마의 전화를 받고 홍은 퍼뜩 스치는 예감이 있었다. "아무개네도 북쪽 여자 데래왔다더라. 저그 둘이서 논밭 쪼매 부치고 시내 나가서 일도 허고, 얼라도 낳고 그래 살믄 되는 기제. 안 글나?" 그전에도 고향마을에 들렀을 적 엄마가 늘 노래처럼 부르던 말이 생각났다.

지병으로 시름시름 앓던 남편을 잃은 지는 십 년도 더 지났고, 요행 별 탈 없이 자라준 맏딸 외에 어려서부터 유약하고 어리숙해 제구실 한번 반듯하게 해내지 못하는 아들을 둔 엄마였다. 겨우 중학을 마치고 여기저기에서 알바나 견습공 노릇을 해오다가 '배 타는 바람'이 불기 시작해서부턴 줄창 배만 타오던 동생 두석은 그때 이미 서른 중반에 다다른 노총각이었으니 어미의 타는 심경은 더 말할 나위가 없는 일이었다.

"엄마는 참, 속 타는 건 알겠는데, 꼭 그렇게까지 해야 돼?" 하고 홍은 한마디 하려다가 그만두었다. 여태 엄마와 자신이 소개해준 여자가 얼마나 많았느냐는 것이며 두석이 녀석 본인은 한 번도 사귀는 친구랍시고 여

ing by. Everything that had happened during that day was also passing by. It was not a bad thing for all things to pass. At any rate, they said the woman had left, hadn't they?

That night, Hong struggled with her lingering feelings about that woman. They wandered through her dreams like they had in other dreams she'd for a few days in a row.

In this last dream, when Hong asked the woman, "Why should I give you the money?" the woman had answered, "Because you have it."

Hong asked her another question. As she did so, though, the woman shifted back and forth from her regular identity into Ok-hwa: "So, I gave you the money. So why are you still not satisfied?" Then the woman looked down at her unsatisfactorily with her slanted eyes, as she had always done in Hong's dreams, and said, "Oh, all *that* money! Money even a dog couldn't use! So you throw a little bit of money at me. No, I'm not grateful! Who do you think you are?"

A little bit of money? How could she say that? Even in her dreams Hong felt so stifled that she rubbed her hand against her chest. "Once I make a lot of money in South Korea, then I won't behave like you guys." After saying that, the woman had

자를 데려온 일이 없었지 않았나 하는 것과 통장에 잔액 몇 푼 없는 집안의 여건 등을 고려해볼 때 그 방법을 나무랄 수만은 없었다.

동생의 뒤를 따라 집 안으로 상큼 들어선 옥화는 비쩍 마른데다가 키도 작아서 아직 발육이 덜 된 중학생처럼 보이는 어린 여자였다. 자기 입으로 스물둘이라고 했지만 스물도 차지 않은 듯 보였다. 동생과는 같은 개띠, 옹근 한 돌림 차이가 났다.

"어떠냐? 맘에 드냐?" 하고 '선'을 주선한 아저씨가 물었을 때 두석은 그냥 헤헤 웃기만 했다고 하였다. "아이구 언니, 말도 말라요. 남자란 게 얼마나 비위가 없는지. 십 분을 앉아 있는데두 암 말 못하는 기라요." 나중에 옥화가 그랬다. 참다 못한 옥화가 먼저 "이름이 뭐이래요?" 물었고 동생이 "김두석이요." 하고 대답했단다. 옥화가 "나이는 얼매래요?" 하면 동생은 "서른넷이요." 했고 "식기는 누기누기 있어요?" 물으면 "내캉 엄마캉 누나 있어요." 하는 식이었단다. 그리고 또 한 십 분 지나서 대단한 용기를 낸 듯 동생이 쭈볏쭈볏거리다 물었단다. "이름이 뭐이요? ……나이는 얼매요? ……식기는 누기누기 있어요?"

grinned at Hong and then in the end doubled over giggling. She then turned into Ok-hwa.

About four or five years ago, Mother, still alive then, had secretly brought a woman home.

"Come on, dear, come quick! Take a look at this girl! She's really nice!" Mother had said, her voice excited, like she had just had bought luxury merchandise at bargain prices in a department store sale.

When she heard her mother's high-pitched voice for the first time in a long while, Hong suddenly remembered what she had said the last time she'd visited her home village: "I heard so-and-so also brought a Northern woman home. If they're able to do a little farming, get a little work downtown, and have a few babies, that's what matters, right?"

Mother had lost her husband more than ten years ago, and had been suffering for a long time. Besides her daughter, who fortunately had grown up without any trouble, she had a son, Du-seok, who'd been weak and childlike and couldn't seem to lead a decent life. After barely managing to finish middle school, he had worked at part-time jobs and as an apprentice here and there, until he became fascinated by seafaring and embarked on that life ever

동생은 옥화를 예뻐했다. 제대로 연애 한 번 못해본 동생은 옥화가 들어오자 화색이 달라졌다. 불밤송이처럼 긴 머리도 깔끔하게 이발했고 사나흘 가도 엄마 잔소리 없으면 갈아입을 궁리 없던 셔츠도 이틀에 한 번 꼴로 바꿔 입었다. 옥화랑 쇼핑 다니면서 보는 눈도 변했는지 값싸고 생기발랄한 티셔츠를 골라 둘이서 사이좋게 사 입고 오기도 했다. 친구들과 술자리에 가서는 예전보다 말도 많아졌고 생전 터뜨려보지 못한 너털웃음으로 친구들을 놀래키기도 했단다.

엄마도 옥화를 안쓰러워했다. 북쪽 어딘가에 있을 친척이 생각나서 그랬을지도 모르겠지만, 엄마는 마음으로 그 아이를 아파했다. "야는 머 먹고 요래빽에 몬 컸노? 갈비빼가 아릉아릉한기 우야다 쓰갔나?" 처음부터 고깃국을 먹지 못하는 옥화에게 엄마는 미음으로 시작해 차차 쌀밥에 가물치에 사골에 우족까지 보신에 좋다는 것은 죄 구하여 먹였다.

물론 홍도 등한시할 수 없었다. 아버지를 일찍 여의고 이 집의 가장이나 다름없이 살아온 홍에게 엄마의 살덩어리인 동생과 같이 살아줄 여자였기에 잘해주고 싶은 마음밖에 없었다. 한 번씩 고향에 내려갈 때마다 고기

since. He was already in his mid-thirties and un-married, so it was understandable that his mother worried and fretted over him and wanted to find him a wife.

"Mom, I understand how anxious you are. But do you really have to do this?" These words were on the tip of Hong's tongue, but she stopped herself. Considering how many women her mother and she had fixed up Du-seok with, how Du-seok had never brought a girlfriend home, and how the family had no balance in their bank account, she couldn't really find fault with her mother's scheme.

Ok-hwa, who readily followed Du-seok into the house, was so thin and small that she looked like a middle-school student. Although she said she was twenty-two, she looked younger than twenty. She was born in the year of dog, so she and Du-seok were twelve years apart.

Hong was told later that her brother had just grinned when the matchmaker uncle asked him, "How do you find her? Do you like her?"

"Goodness, Sister, what can I say? He was so shy. He didn't say a word for ten minutes," Ok-hwa had told Hong later.

So when impatient Ok-hwa asked him, "What's your name?" he answered, "Kim Du-seok."

면 고기, 귀한 과일이면 과일, 옷이면 옷, 책이면 책, 용
돈은 물론이고 최신형 휴대폰에 엠피스리까지, 해줄 수
있는 것, 옥화가 부러워하는 티라도 보인 적 있는 것이
면 어떻게든 마련해보려고 애썼던 홍이다.

그런데, 어떻게 그렇게 말할 수가 있지? 그 잘난 돈?
그까짓 거 해줬다고? 꿈속에서 여자는 그렇게 웃다가
갑자기 연기처럼 사라지고 홍은 혼자 갈대밭을 헤매고
걷고 있었다. 대체 뭐가 불만이야? 그렇게 해준 게 잘못
이란 말인가? 얼마나 더 해줘야 한단 말인가?

"집사님, 내 아무리 궁리해두 집사님 얼굴 한번 보고
가야갔시요." 돈을 준 뒤, 여자가 떠나갔다는 소식을 듣
기 며칠 전의 어느날, 홍은 여자에게서 온 연락을 받았
다. 그 정 떨어지는 듯한 까칠한 억양을 듣는 순간, 홍은
머리가 지끈거려왔다. 또 무엇인가. 받아 가졌으면 그
만이지, 무슨 할 말이 또 남았는가. 어렵사리 돈을 주고
도 고까운 책망이나 받을 것 같다는 예감에, 홍은 애써
정리한 옷장이 뒤집혔을 때처럼 속이 부글거리기 시작
했다. 그래서 "아저씨, 한두 번 해본 일도 아니면서 왜
그래요!" 하고 금방 배송 갔다 오는 기사 아저씨한테 노

When Ok-hwa asked, "How old are you?" he answered, "Thirty-four."

And when Ok-hwa asked, "Who's in your family?" he answered, "Me, mom, and sister."

Then, after about ten minutes, after mustering all of his courage, Du-seok asked her, "What's your name? How old are you? Who's in your family?" That was what Ok-hwa had recounted.

Du-seok loved Ok-hwa. He had never even had a girlfriend. As soon as Ok-hwa joined the family, Du-seok's face turned ruddy. He had his chestnut burr hair tidily cut, and he began to change his shirt every other day, unlike before when he might have changed it every several days, and then only because of his mother's nagging. When they went out shopping together, they came back wearing cheap but vivid-colored T-shirts they had bought together, perhaps because his taste had changed thanks to Ok-hwa. When he was out drinking with his friends Du-seok became talkative, and he surprised his friends with laughter that they had never heard from him before. Mother took pity on Ok-hwa, too. Perhaps because she reminded mother of her relatives living somewhere in North Korea, mother felt for her from the bottom of her heart.

"Whatever did she eat? How come she's so small?

골적으로 화를 박박 내기도 했다.

"적반하장도 유분수지. 제가 어쩌면 그럴수 있을까."
한 번씩 푸념 삼아 철없는 옥화의 얘기를 꺼내는 엄마
와 통화할 때 홍이 가끔 하던 말이었다. 엄마가 본 것처
럼 그 아이는 똑똑하고 야무졌다. 몸을 추스리고 나서
는 동네 산책도 다니고 동생이랑 시내에 쇼핑도 다니면
서 식견을 넓힌 그녀는 아무도 가르쳐주지 않았는데 혼
자 한문을 익히고 컴퓨터도 동생 등 너머로 찔끔찔끔
배웠다. 급기야 동생이 배 타러 떠난 뒤엔 엄마의 약값
벌이를 핑계로 취직시켜 달라고 이틀이 멀다 하고 홍에
게 졸랐다. "내 이리 젊은 게 집에서 놀믄 뭐한대요? 내
두 쫌 벌어 보태야디요."

주위에서는 홍을 말렸다. "처음엔 취직이지? 그다음
엔 가출이야. 동생 들어오면 애나 빨리 만들라고 해." 홍
도 걱정이 안되는 게 아니었다. 엄마가 늘 부러워하던
아무개네 며느리를 포함한 동네 몇몇 북녘여자들 태반
이 어느날 갑자기 행방이 묘연해졌다는 소문이 퍼지고
있었는데 개중에는 돌을 갓 넘긴 핏덩어리를 내치고 떠
난 이도 있다는 말을 전해들었기 때문이었다.

게다가 옥화의 소행도 홍의 귀에 벌써 몇 건 흘러들

You can almost see her ribs. What can she do with that body?" Mother said and then fed Ok-hwa, who couldn't eat meat soup. Instead she fed her everything that was supposedly good for one's health, beginning with rice water and moving to boiled rice, snakeheaded fish, and then cow bone soup.

Hong, who had been living as the practical head of the household couldn't neglect Ok-kwa either. Hong only wanted to do well by her, because she was going to live with her brother, the apple of her mother's eye. Whenever Ok-hwa visited her home village, Hong tried to get her everything she appeared to envy and like, from the newest model cell phone to an MP3 player, to meat, rare fruit, clothes, books, and pocket money that she showered on her.

After all that, how could Ok-hwa have said all those aggressive things to Hong? All that money! A little bit of money? In her dreams Ok-hwa laughed and then disappeared, and Hong continued to wander in a reed field. What on earth was she not satisfied with? Was it wrong to be generous to her? What more should Hong have done for her?

"Madam Deacon, I thought and thought it over, but I really have to see you before I leave," the

어와 있던 차였다. 절름발이 윤아저씨네 슈퍼에 엄마 이름으로 달아놓은 외상이며 국숫집 이아저씨한테서는 아르바이트비를 선불로 당겨써서 되려 빚만 쌓였다는 등등의 일은 심기가 언짢아지는 일이었지만 그때까지는 매번 엄마와 상의해서 좋게 얘기하고 넘겼다.

그래도 설마 하는 마음에 결국 홍은 옥화의 청을 끝까지 뿌리치지 못했다. 하여 일 년 가까이 옥화는 홍네 집에서 기거하며 식당이나 가게에서 두루 일했고 주일에 쉴 때가 있으면 홍을 따라 교회 예배에 나가기도 하였다. 어느날 갑자기 편지 한 장 달랑 남겨놓고 떠나가기 전까지…….

"내 솔찍히 여기서 좋은 사람들 많이 만났시요. 그만하믄 잘해줬디요. 모두 바쁘게 사는 사람들인데……." 전화로 여자가 말했다. 그러나 홍의 귀에는 그 말들이 진정 고맙다는 인사로 들리지 않았다. '그만하믄'이라니? 그럼 얼마나 더 베풀어주어야 한단 말인가? 왜 이 사람들은 베풂을 한낱 당연한 것으로 생각한단 말인가? 꿈속 여자의 말처럼 단지 '가졌다'는 것이 그 이유가 될 수 있단 말인가?

woman had told her on the phone a few days before Hong heard the news about her departure.

The moment she heard that voice, dry and curt,
Hong felt a headache. What more did she want?
She'd gotten what she wanted, so what more did
she have to say? Hong anticipated some sort of
spiteful reproach after giving her hard-earned
money, and began to feel her stomach churning, as
if a pair of just-tidied drawers had been over-
turned.

All of this was why Hong exploded when her
store's driver returned from his delivery: "Hey, this
isn't your first or second time delivering, right?"

"How brazen she was! How could she say that to
us?" was Hong's response to her mother's occa-
sional complaints about the childish Ok-hwa.

Mom was right about how smart and clever Ok-
hwa was. After she recovered from her past ordeal
before arriving at my mother's house, Ok-hwa began to expand her knowledge just walking around
the village and shopping with Hong's brother
downtown. She learned Chinese, although nobody
had taught her. She also developed computer skills
just by looking over Du-seok's shoulders. Then, finally, after Du-seok left for overseas, she began to
pester Hong, asking her to find her a job, her ex-

여자의 전화를 받으면서 홍은 옥화의 눈빛을 떠올렸다. 슈퍼집 외상이나 국수집 빚이나 홍네 거실 책상 위에서 사라진 돈푼들을 물을 때, 옥화는 당당하게 대답했었다. "그거이요? 맞아요, 내가 그랬시요." 옥화의 눈빛은 너무나 당당해서, 마치 그 돈의 행방을 묻고 있는 홍 자신이 천박하고 죄스럽게 느껴질 정도였다. 어처구니없어하는 남편의 불쾌감과 그까짓 것 가지고 힐문한다고 생각하는 듯한 옥화의 고까움 사이에서 홍의 스트레스는 점점 한계로 치달아올랐다. 자연 옥화에 대한 동정과 이해보다는 짜증과 미움이 날로 커져가서 무의식 중 그녀를 대하는 언행 속에 그 속마음이 나타났을 것이다.

그것은, 여자의 궁한 처지가 딱해서 같이 밥이라도 먹으며 도울 수 있는 방법을 알아보자고까지 마음먹었다가, 그날 자동현금지급기 앞에서 그만 그 마음을 온데간데없이 잃어버렸던 경우와 마냥 흡사했다. "자매님, 저 이런 소리는 정말 하지 않을려구 했는데요. 글쎄 자매님한테는 이 돈이 얼마나 도움이 되는지 모르겠지만, 저한테도 쉬운 일은 아니거든요. 사정 얘기 다 하면 뭐 끝도 없고, 이해도 잘 안 되실 거고, 그래서 여하튼 사천

cuse being that she wanted to make money for her mother's medicine.

"A young woman like me, what am I doing at home, idly whiling away all my time? I should make money and help with the household."

Neighbors told Hong not to listen to it, saying, "At first, it's a job. But then, the next thing she's going to do is run away! Just wait until your brother comes back. Tell him to make a baby quick!"

Hong was herself worried. Rumor had it that most North Korean women, including the daughter-in-law of so-and-so, whom Mom always envied, had suddenly disappeared. It was said that some of them even ran away after leaving a one-year-old child.

Besides, Ok-hwa had already shown a number of troubling behaviors. She bought things on credit from the Cripple Yun's supermarket using mom's name. She also received advance payment for her part-time work at Mr. Yi's noodle shop, and accumulated debts. Although Hong was unhappy about these incidents, she would talk it over with her mother and solve the problems Ok-hwa had created.

Still, not wanting to doubt her, Hong couldn't refuse Ok-hwa's entreaties in the end. So for about a

은 안 되겠고 삼천만 해드릴게요. 갚으려고 생각지는 마세요..제가 뭐, 이거 되받으려고 주는 게 아니니까."

옥화의 모습이 자꾸 연상되어서일까, 홍은 그날 여자한테 울분 비슷하게 언성을 높여 그간 불편했던 속을 쏟아내고 말았다. 기계가 뱉어낸 빨간 지폐 삼십 장을 세서 봉투에 넣어 건네주었을 때 여자는 구푸렸던 허리에서 손을 떼고 곧게 서 있었다. 여자는 아무 말도 하지 않고 봉투를 받아 가방에 주워넣었다. 홍은 그 얼굴을 슬쩍 훔쳐보고 싶다는 충동을 느꼈지만 그러면 또다시 마음이 약해질 것 같아서 꾹 참았다. 홍이 먼저 돌아섰던가, 여자가 홍의 등뒤에서 조그맣게 "고맙다요, 집사님." 하고 인사하는 말을 들었다.

자존심이었을까? 그네들이 그렇게 사실적으로 도움을 받고도 결코 고맙다고 얘기할 수 없는 것은 혹시 상처받은 자존심 때문이었을까? "뭐 군이 다시 볼 일이 뭐가 있겠어요? 자매님이나 무사하게 잘 가시면 되는 거죠." 하고 홍이 극력 말리는 말에 여자는, "아니라요, 내쪼꿈만 집사님 보고 올 테니게, 상점에서 기다리시라요. 내 집사님 안 보고 가는 날에는, 가도 내 속이 절대 안 내래갈 거 같다요." 하는 식으로 부득부득 우겼다.

year, Ok-hwa lived at Hong's house and worked in various restaurants and shops. On Sundays, Ok-hwa also accompanied Hong to church if it was her day off. But then, one day, she suddenly ran away, leaving behind nothing but a single letter.

"Honestly, I met many good people here. They were all pretty generous. I know you all work hard and it's not easy to make a living," the woman said on the phone.

To Hong, though, it still didn't seem like she was telling her that she was truly grateful. "Pretty generous"? So what more did we have to do for them? Why did they take our generosity for granted? As the woman had said in her dream, could "because you have it" be reason enough?

Listening to her on the phone, Hong remembered Ok-hwa's eyes. When Ok-hwa had been interrogated about the credit at the supermarket, her debt to the noodle shop, or the money that had disappeared from the desk in the living room, she had said, unfazed, "Oh, that? That's right. I did that."

The look in Ok-hwa's eyes was so righteous that they almost made Hong feel superficial and guilty. Between her husband's displeasure and Ok-hwa's reproach toward what she perceived as Hong's petti-

그리하여 마지막으로 여자를 보았던 그날은, 마침 삼사 년 족히 보지 못한 시형(媤兄)이 한국에서 돌아온 날이었다. 원체 농사만 짓고 살던 위인이라 까무잡잡했던 시형의 얼굴은 그새 거짓말처럼 때물을 쑥 벗고 허여멀쑥하니 변해 있었다. "어쨌든 물은 그쪽이 좋은가벼." 남편과 시형이 가게 부근의 식당에서 권커니 잣거니 술을 마시는 동안 홍은 이제 곧 들이닥칠 여자의 시답지 않은 방문을 기다렸다. "그래, 그쪽에서 영 눌러살던 사람들도 많던데, 형님은 어떻소?" 남편이 묻는 말에 시형은 독한 술을 한 모금 들이켜고는 절레절레 손을 내둘렀다. 거개가 거기서 거기인 얘기들이었다. 힘든 노동, 사람들의 배척과 편견, 보장받지 못하는 인권……. 그리하여 그곳에서의 정착은 아직 미래가 명랑하지 못하다는 게 타국에서 일하는 모든 이국 노무자들의 결론이었다.

시형이 풀어내는 긴 이야기를 들어주는 동안에 여자에게서 버스터미널 이름을 확인하는 전화가 왔다. 옥화처럼 여자도 한문을 웬만큼 익히고 있었던 모양이었다. "에이, 못사는 게 죄지. 잘사는 나라에 살지 않는다고 대우가 이렇게 다르니……." 술에 약한 시형은 간만에 많이 마셔서 혀를 잘 굴리지도 못했다. 오랜만에 혈육을

ness, Hong was getting terribly stressed. Quite naturally, her annoyance and hatred toward Ok-hwa were growing larger than her sympathy for and understanding of her. Ok-hwa should have perceived this from Hong's attitude.

A similar situation happened when Hong, after resolving to discuss how to help the woman out of sympathy for her situation, completely lost her desire to help her in front of the ATM.

"Sister, I really didn't mean to say this to you, but saving this much money really isn't easy for me, although I'm not sure how helpful it would be to you. It's a long story and I don't know if you can even understand. But, at any rate, I'll give you 3,000 instead of 4,000 *won*. You don't have to repay me. I'm not giving this to you to get it back," Hong had said.

Perhaps, because the woman had reminded Hong of Ok-hwa she'd said all of this? Hong had ended up pouring out all her feelings, loudly and almost angrily. When Hong handed her 30 red bills spit out by the machine, after counting and putting them in an envelope, the woman was standing straight now and no longer rubbing her bent back. Without a word, the woman received the envelope and placed it inside her purse. Hong felt the impulse to look her in the face, but refrained from

만난 남편도 한마디 거들고 나섰다. "이제 우리두 잘살
아보우. 그땐 형편이 영 달라집지."

"그러게 속담에 용꼬리보다 닭대가리라 했나? 야, 이
번 여름에 너 형수랑 같이 들어와선, 우리도 그 뭐냐 가
족으로다 여행 가자. 응? 제수씨, 거 왜, 가난하고 멋있
는 동네 많잖아요. 거기 가서 우리도 돈 한번 써보자요.
흐흐." 말수가 항상 많지 않던 시형은 그날 갑자기 마셔
버린 독한 술을 미처 소화하지 못해서인지 여느때보다
발랄하게 취해 있었다.

우체국 역에 도착했다는 여자의 전화를 받고 나오면
서 홍은 시형의 벌겋게 취한 얼굴을 생각해보았다. 눈
만 뜨면 일, 일 하는 것 외에 그 나라 일반 국민이 누릴
수 있는 어떤 것도 누릴 수 없는 돈벌이 기계 같은 생활
들, 그곳에서 시형네는 몸뚱이 하나와 불법체류자의 신
분 외에 아무것도 가진 것이 없는 사람들이었다. 여자
처럼? 옥화처럼?

아무도 알지 못하고 아무도 믿을 수 없는 상황에서
시형네는 어디를 가나 누구를 만나나 자신들의 진실한
이야기를 꺼내놓을 수가 없었다고 했다. "사람이 말이
야, 그 상황에 들어가니까 그렇게 되더라고. 자기는 안

doing so, afraid that she would lose her resolve. Perhaps it was Hong who turned around first. She could hear the woman softly say behind her, "Thank you, Madam Deacon."

Was it their pride? Were they unable to say thank you after receiving such practical aid because of their wounded pride?

"Is there any reason we should meet again? I just hope you get to South Korea safely," Hong insisted.

But the woman insisted even more emphatically, "No, please. I'll just drop by your store to see you. Please wait in the store. If I go without seeing you, I'll never feel comfortable about myself."

It so happened that the last time Hong saw her was the day when her brother-in-law, whom she hadn't seen for several years, returned from South Korea. His face, which had once been deeply tanned from farming, had changed completely. Unbelievably, he was now light-skinned.

"At any rate, the water must be better in Korea than here," Hong's husband had said.

While Hong's husband and brother-in-law were drinking at a restaurant near the store, Hong reluctantly waited for the woman's visit, listening to their conversation.

그럴 것 같지? 흐흐. 아니야. 사람은 다 같애." 시형의 발
랄한 웃음 속에서 홍은 자기편이 아닌 땅에서 살아가는
이들의 불안함을 보았다.

"언니, 내두 알아요. 언니랑 어머이랑 내게 얼매나 잘
했는지 알아요. 내는 머 암것두 한 게 없다는 거이두 알
아요. 내가 가믄 원망 많이 듣겠다는 거두 알아요. 기래
두 나는 가야 돼요." 옥화는 편지에 자신이 반드시 떠나
야 하는 이유를 명확히 적어놓지 않았다. 옥화는 그 동
네에서 마지막으로 '떠나가버린' 북녘 여자였다. 그 여
자들 모두 옥화처럼 가야 하는 이유를 아무한테도 말해
본 적이 없었다. 조국에서 중국으로, 중국에서 다시 한
국으로……. 그저 떠나가는 게 그들의 바람이었단 말
인가.

어쩌면, 하고 홍은 터미널에 서 있는 여자를 향해 손
을 흔들어 보였다. 여자도 홍을 알아보고 행인들 속을
헤치면서 그녀에게로 다가왔다. 초행길이라 그랬을까,
낯선 중국인 무리에 끼인 여자는 가방을 두 손으로 부
여잡은 채 온몸이 경직된 채로 걸어오고 있었다. 어쩌
면 그런 불안감 때문에 그들은 떠날 수밖에 없었던 것
인가. 다시는 불안하지 않을 곳으로…….

"So, there seem to be many people who've decided to settle there. What's your plan, Big Brother?" Hong's husband had said.

Hong's brother-in-law drank a sip of hard liquor and waved repeatedly. His stories were much the same as other people's: hard labor, exclusion and prejudice, human rights violations, and so on. His conclusion was the same as the other migrant workers: the prospect of future settlements was not quite bright yet.

While listening to her brother-in-law's long diatribe, Hong received a call from the woman confirming the name of the bus terminal. Like Ok-hwa, the woman must have learned some Chinese.

"Huh, to be poor is to be guilty. Look how differently they treat you just because you're from a poor country!" Hong's brother-in-law couldn't drink well and his words slurred a little.

"Let's wait and see. Once we're rich, they'll treat us differently," Hong's husband rejoined, encouraging his brother, whom he was glad to see after so long.

"Isn't there a saying that it's better to be a chicken head than a dragon tail? Hey, I'll visit this summer with my wife. Then let's go on a—what do you call it—*family trip*. Okay? Sister-in-law, aren't there a

홍은 여자를 데리고 부근의 대형 지하할인마트로 갔
다. 간식거리도 사 먹을 수 있고 다리쉼도 할 수 있는 간
이의자가 많이 놓인 공간이 거기에 있었다. "집사님, 미
안해요. 바쁜데 우정 나오라구 기래서……" 맨입으로
앉아 있기 뭐해 과자나 주스라도 사오려는 홍을 향해
여자는 눈썹을 찌푸리며 완고하게 손을 내둘렀다. "아
니라요. 내는 목도 안 마르고 안 먹어도 돼요. 씰데없는
돈 쓰지 말라요." 여자가 주위 사람 보기 민망할 정도로
팔을 억세게 잡아끄는 바람에 홍은 하는 수 없이 겨우
일회용 플라스틱컵에 담긴 오렌지주스를 두 잔 시켜놓
고 여자와 소심하게 마주 앉았다.

"내 이제 낼모레쯤이믄 한국으로 떠날 거 같애요." 한
참 어색한 침묵이 흐른 뒤, 여자가 입을 열었다. "사람들
은 여기서 일도 하고 맘에 맞는 사람 만나 살라디만, 긴
데 기실 여기서는 하고 싶은 거 아무거이두 못해요. 거
기 가므느 합법적으루 뭐이나 할 수 있대니, 가야디요."
여자가 한 모금 빨고 내려놓은 컵 벽에서 주스가 주르
륵 흘러내렸다. 물은 어쩔 수 없이 아래로 흐르는 법, 홍
도 말없이 주스를 들이켰다.

"그날 집사님 얼굴을 보니께네 내 속이 속이 아니래

lot of poor, but nice scenic villages? Let's go there and spend some money. Ha-ha." Hong's brother-in-law, usually quiet, had become talkative, probably because he had gotten drunk from the hard liquor, which he must have had for the first time in a while.

Hong left the restaurant after receiving a call from the woman and made her way to the Post Office station. Hong thought of her brother-in-law's flushed face. In a country where he and his wife worked like moneymaking machines, unable to enjoy anything South Koreans could, they were people who owned nothing other than their bodies and their illegal alien status. Like the woman. Or perhaps even Ok-hwa?

In that country, where they neither knew nor trusted anybody, her brother-in-law said that they couldn't tell their true stories to anybody anywhere.

"Once you're in that situation, you know, you just become like that. You think you won't? No. Everyone's the same," Hong's brother-in-law said, laughing. In her brother-in-law's raucous laughter, Hong could feel the anxiety of all those who lived in the land of people not on their side.

"Sister, I know very well. You and Mother were all very generous to me. I also know that I did

서요." 하고 문득 여자가 눈을 들어 홍을 쳐다보았다. 순간 그 눈에서 푸른빛이 번뜩 나오는 듯하여 차라리 쏘아보는 것처럼 느껴졌다. "내 집에 가서 자는디, 암만 해도 잠이 오디를 않았시요."

홍은 휴지를 찾기 위해 머리를 수굿하고 가방 안을 들여다보았다. 여자의 집요한 눈초리가 자신의 이마 부근에 머물고 있다는 게 느껴져서 심히 불편했다. 이제 시작인가. 왜 나인가. 왜 내가 이런 말들을 들어야 하는가?

"내 지금 집사님보구 머라구 하는 거 아니라요, 내는 그 기도모임에 나가서 집사님 알았디요. 말하는 거이랑 가마이 들어보니께네 하느님께 믿음도 좋고 사람도 참 좋은 사람이다 싶더라요. 기래서 집사님 정도믄 내를 쫌 이해해주시갔나 했디요."

여자의 억양은, "언니, 맞아요. 그거이 내가 기랬시요." 하던 옥화의 목소리처럼 정당하게 들리고 있었다. 홍은 그 말을 하는 옥화의 맑은 눈빛 속에서 그 아이가 자신에 대해 지나친 믿음 같은 것을 지니고 있다는 것을 보아내고 깜짝 놀랐었다. 옥화는 무슨 배짱으로 홍을 그렇게 믿을 수 있었으며 그렇게 믿었던 홍에게 힐문을

nothing. I know that I'll be blamed if I leave. Still, I have to go."

Ok-hwa hadn't clarified why she had to go in her letter. Ok-hwa was the last North Korean woman who had left Hong's village. No North Korean women clarified their reason to anyone. From their fatherland to China, from China to South Korea... Was it their wish to simply leave?

Maybe. Hong saw the woman standing in the terminal and waved. The woman recognized Hong, too, and pushed through the people towards her. The woman looked tense, walking toward Hong and holding her bag tight and close to her body with both hands. Was it because it was her first trip? Perhaps, because of their anxiety, they had to leave? To get to a place where they wouldn't feel that way again?

Hong took her to the large basement discount store nearby. There was a space with many chairs where they could get snacks and sit.

"I'm sorry, Madam Deacon, for calling you out when you're busy," the woman said and waved her hand stubbornly, to tell Hong not to buy cookies or juice. Hong was about to purchase some to avoid any awkwardness. "No. I'm not thirsty and I don't need to eat. Please don't waste your money

받고 고깝다고 생각하기에 이르렀을까.

"긴데 왜 집사님은 딴 사람들 말으 듣고 내를 기래 생
각하는디, 속에 점말 안 내래갔시요." 정말 밤잠을 설쳐
서인지 여자의 목소리는 점점 갈리고 있었다. "내도 그
만한 눈치는 있디요. 집사님 머라 안 기캐도 내 대하는
얼굴 보니께니 이거이 무슨 안 좋은 말으 들었다 싶었
디요. 긴데, 그 사람들 누기 하나 내를 아는 사람이 있시
요? 내 머 이 교회 이 년 다녔다 기캐두, 무스 하느님 그
런 거이도 잘 모르고 사람들도 잘 모르고, 또 그 사람들
도 내를 잘 몰라요. 기래, 머 쌀이나 김치나 그런 거이는
잘 갖다줬디요, 내 혼자 먹으므 얼매 먹는다고……. 좌
우간 굶지는 않았디요. 일자리도 마니 알아바주고 했시
요. 내가 이 허리만 안 아프믄 무스 그런 거이 가리고 하
겠시요? 내 주제가 머 이거저거 가릴 주제나 되갔시
요?"

열렬한 열변을 토하느라 여자의 시선은 홍의 이마에
서 어느새 옮겨간 것 같았다. 그제야 홍은 슬쩍 눈을 들
어 여자의 얼굴을 훔쳐볼 수 있었다. 여자는 매장의 구
석, 아직 인테리어를 하지 않아 정전이 된 어두운 벽쪽
을 쳐다보며 혼자 코웃음을 흥흥 치고 있었다. 그 어둠

on me."

Because she had dragged Hong's arms almost embarrassingly, Hong sat across from her after ordering only two plastic cups of orange juice.

"I think I'll leave for South Korea in a day or two," the woman said after a long, awkward silence. "People told me to marry and just look for any kind of job here, but I can do nothing I want here. Since I heard that I could do anything legally there, I have to go." A drop of juice trickled down the side of the woman's cup. Water cannot help but to flow downward, Hong thought. Hong drank her juice without saying another word.

"After looking at your face that day, I didn't feel comfortable at all," the woman said and suddenly looked up at Hong. Her eyes seemed to shoot out brilliant rays. Hong felt as if she was being glared at. "I went back home and went to bed, but I couldn't sleep."

Hong looked inside her bag for a napkin. She could feel the woman's persistent glance at her own forehead. It was quite uncomfortable. Was this the beginning of some sort of interrogation? Why me? Why should I hear this?

"I'm not blaming you, Madam Deacon. During the prayer meeting, I got to know you. Listening to

속에서 마치 어떤 무리를 실제로 보아내기라도 한 듯이.

"집사님은 내가 어떠케래 여기까정 왔는디 모르디 요?" 비어가는 컵을 쥔 여자의 손이 그 말을 할 때 간간 히 떨렸다.

"언니, 우리 집에는 아(兒)들이 너이 있었시요. 우에는 언니 둘이, 내 밑으루 남동생 하나." 자매 둘만 있었다며 가족들 상황은 항상 어물어물 넘겨버리곤 하던 옥화는 마지막 남겨놓은 편지에 그리 썼다. "언니 둘이는 시 집 갔디요, 먹을 거나 잘 먹고 사는디, 발써 굶어죽었는 지도 모르갔고, 남동생은 아직 너무 작아서 머 일으 못 시켜먹고⋯⋯. 기래서 내가 먹을 거 구해볼라구 나왔 시요."

여자는 이제 덤덤해진 눈길로 홍을 건너다보았다. 가 장 신랄한 신세 얘기를 꺼낼 때, 여자의 눈빛 속에는 오 히려 값싼 슬픔이나 비애 같은 것이 들어 있지 않았다. "⋯⋯두만강 혜엄채 건너와가지고 사람 장사꾼한테 붙 잡했디요. 인자는 그 사람들도 이력이 나서 엔벤이나 조선족 동네에다 안 팔고 내를 저 하북성 산골 오지에 다 팔더래요. 집이라고는 사방 벽에 지붕이라고 대수 걸채 놓은데다가, 남자라고는 맨날 일도 못하고 헤벌써

what you said, I thought that you were a true believer and a good person. So, I thought you'd understand me."

The woman's voice indicated that same pride that Hong had heard from Ok-hwa when she said, "Sister, that's right. I did that." Hong had been surprised then to see how clear Ok-hwa's eyes were, the total trust in Hong. How could Ok-hwa trust Hong so much and how could she find Hong's inquisition so shameful?

"But, then, how could you listen to others and think so ill of me – I thought about it, but I couldn't take it." Her voice was getting lower and huskier, probably because she really hadn't been able to sleep.

"I could see—even before you said anything, I could see from your face that you heard other people speak ill of me. But did any of them really know me? Even though I attended the church for two years, I still don't know much about God or other people. And they don't know much about me either. True, they did give me things like rice and *kimchi*. I was the only one eating, so how much could I eat, right? I didn't starve. Sure, they found me a lot of jobs, but if I didn't have this back pain, why would I have refused them? I wasn't in the

죽채 있는 게……. 거기서 내 혼자 농사짓고 돼지 치고, 살림하고, 그저 죽게 일하고 살았디요. 애새끼도 하나 낳았시요." 여자는 막 말을 배우기 시작한 두 살배기 아들을 늙은 노파와 모자란 남정에게 남겨두고 신새벽 어둠을 타서 도보로 이틀길을 걸어 가장 가까운 기차역까지 나갔다고 했다. 기차에서 우연히 내린 곳이 이 도시였고 정처없이 걷다가 지쳐 쓰러진 곳이 교회 부근인 모양이었다.

"내가 어떤 사람인지 아시갔어요? 내는 내 뱃속으로 낳은 내 아새끼도 내삐리고 도망친 사람이라요. 더 말해 머하갔시요?" 이 말을 뱉고 나서야 비로소 여자는 눈에서 힘을 뺐다. 여자의 안확 안에서 맑은 액체 같은 것이 순간 조용히 솟구치려다 말았다. "어머이랑 언니랑 내한테 정말 잘해주셨다는 거 압니다. 그것도 모르는 사람은 아닙니다……." 옥화의 편지에서 그 구절을 읽으며 홍은 상처난 자리에 소금이 뿌려진 듯 마음이 쓰라렸었다.

"내는 머 목사가 맨날 말하는 믿음이란 게 어떤 거인디 그딴 거 잘 모르는데, 기래도 이거는 압네다. 한 사람이 어떻다는 거이는 하느님만 아시디, 딴 사람들으는

position to be choosy, right?"

During this oration, the woman's glance seemed to have moved away from Hong's forehead. Hong was finally able to look up and steal a glance at the woman's face. She looked contemptuous, staring out in the direction of a dark wall that hadn't been decorated yet. She looked as if she was seeing a certain group of people within that darkness.

"You don't know how I ended up here, do you?" The woman's hands holding her cup trembled a little.

"Sister, our family has four children. I have two elder sisters and a younger brother," Ok-hwa had written in the letter she'd left. She used to go back and forth about her family, and had said she just had the one sister. "Both elder sisters married. I wonder if they have enough to eat. They might have starved to death by now. My brother is too young to work...That's why I came here. To get food."

The woman was looking at Hong now, much more calmly. She was talking about the bitterest facts of her life, but her eyes didn't show any melodramatic anguish or pathos.

"After I had swam across the Duman River, I was captured by human traffickers. They were veterans.

다 모른다는 거이요. 안 기래요, 집사님?" 한 밀차 가득
물건을 실은 젊은 부부가 매장에서 나와 그녀들 곁을
지나쳤다. 젊고 건강하고 배울 만큼 배워 보이는, 가진
게 많아 보이는 사람들이었다. 시형 말처럼 다 같은 사
람들이라면, 저 사람들이 소유한 그 많은 것들은 모두
어디서 온 것이란 말인가?

 "내는 머 교회 사람들이는 머가 달라도 달른가 했디
요." 잠시 눈을 파는 사이, 여자의 목소리가 다시 홍의
귀를 때렸다. 교회 사람들이라니? 아니, 교회 사람들은
무엇을 가졌기에 다르다고 생각했을까? '믿음'을 말하는
건가? "……마지막에는 내를 중간에 앉해놓고 위원인
가 머인가 하는 령도들이 쭉 둘러앉아서 죄인 심판하듯
이 심판합데다. 너는 이래서 아이되고, 너는 이래서 어
쩌고……. 그 최권산가 먼가 하는 할마이는, 기래, 그
할마이가 쌀도 웰 마니 주긴 줬디, 길쎄 나르 보고 하느
님도 싫어할 사람이라고 합데다."

 젊은 부부의 묵직한 밀차가 한창 '없는 사람들' 무리를
헤집고 있었다. 부유하고, 학식있고, 덕망있고……. 또
'믿음' 있는 사람들에게 둘러싸여 죄인이 된 그날의 여
자가 눈앞에 보이는 듯하였다. 그래서 여자가 받은 것

They didn't sell North Koreans to Yanbian or ethnic Korean villages. They sold them to remote mountain villages. The shack I lived in was just a rough roof over four walls, and the man was unable to work and just laid around all day...I worked the farm, raised the pigs, and did the housework all by myself. I worked like hell, and had a baby, too."

She said that she had run away, leaving behind her two-year old son, who had just begun speaking, his grandmother, and the disabled father. She walked day and night for two days until she got to the nearest train station. She happened to get off in this city and walked on until she was so exhausted that she collapsed near the church.

"Do you now understand who I am? I ran away. I deserted my own baby. What more can I say about myself?" It was only after saying this that her eyes became gentle. Clear pools stopped just short of springing out of her eyes.

"I know Mother and you both did well by me. I'm not the kind of person who doesn't recognize that." When Hong had read those sentences in Ok-hwa's letter, it was so painful that it felt like salt was rubbed into her wound.

"I don't know what the belief the pastor sings praises of everyday is, but I know this: only God

들이 '그 잘란 것, 그딴 거' 따위가 되었단 말인가? 텅 빈 주스컵이 결국 속 보이는 얇다란 플라스틱통이 되어 홍의 손안에서 푹 물앉아버렸다.

"집사님이 내를 방조한 거, 내 까먹지 않는다요. 내 이 땀에 돈 많이 벌믄, 꼭 갚을 거라요. 기리구 나는 잘살믄……." 여자는 거기까지 얘기하고 더 하지 않았다. 애초부터 되돌려받으려고 준 돈이 아니라고, 진심으로 그저 여자가 무사하기만 바란다고 홍이 재차 말해주어도 소용없었다. 그같은 상황에서는 여자더러 갚으라고 하는 것이 오히려 그녀를 존중해주는 일인 듯싶었다.

여자는 자신이 오던 대로 우체국 역에 가서 반대방향으로 가는 버스를 기다렸다. "내 여직꺼정 누기보구 이런 얘기 해보디르 않았는디, 집사님보구 내 얘기 다 하니께네 인자 내 속이 편안해요." 버스에 오르기 전, 여자가 모처럼 잠깐 얼굴을 펴 보였다.

그러나 여자를 태운 버스가 기우뚱거리며 출발할 때 홍은 그 버스가 뿜어내는 검은 매연에 눈이 매워났다. "기리구 나는 잘살믄 당신들처럼 안 기래요……." 여자가 뿜어내고 싶었던 마지막 말은 그것이었을까? 그런데 그것은 정말 여자 자신이 말했던 것처럼, 하느님만 아시

and no one else that can understand a person. Isn't that true, Madam Deacon?"

A young couple left the store pushing a cart and passed them. They looked young, healthy, and intelligent. They looked like they owned all sorts of things. If every human being is the same, as Hong's brother-in-law had said, where did all those things the young people owned come from?

"I thought that Christians would be different from other people," the woman's voice cut through Hong's thoughts again. Christians? What made her think that Christians should have been different from others? Because they had "beliefs"?

"In the end, the so-called leaders sat around me at the center and acted as if they were interrogating a criminal. You shouldn't do this. You're so-and-so, because you did that...That grandma Exhorter Choi, huh! True, she gave me a lot of rice. That woman called me a person even God would hate."

The heavy cart the young couple was pushing was in the middle of a crowd of "have-nots." Hong could see the woman as a criminal surrounded by those who were wealthy, intelligent, and virtuous... believers. Was that why what she received from them had become "those great things, whatever"?

는 일이 아닐까? 차창 곁에 앉은 여자의 태연한 옆모습을 올려다보면서 홍은 혼자 남아 쿨럭쿨럭 기침했다.

아침이 밝아 눈을 뜨고 일어나 앉는다. 자정을 넘겨 들어왔는지, 새벽녘에 들어왔는지, 바로 곁에서 남편이 술냄새를 지독하게 피우며 쓰러져 자고 있다. 어제 또 기사 아저씨랑 같이 물건을 날랐는가, 이마를 짚고 있는 손등에 새로 긁힌 벌건 흔적들이 여기저기 보인다. 무거운 마루자재를 나르랴, 수금날 전에 미리 사장들을 접대하랴, 어지간히 피곤했을 것이다. 이 집의 가장이고 여남은 되는 직원들의 책임자가 아니던가.

남편 곁을 살그머니 떠나 거실에 있는 시계를 보니, 2013년 10월 27일 수요일이다. 오늘은 무슨 일이 있더라도 기도모임에 가야겠다고 홍은 마음먹는다. 아들을 위해서 남편을 위해서 가게를 위해서, 그리고 길을 떠난 여자의 안전을 위해서.

서둘러 밥솥에 쌀을 씻어 안치며 된장국이나 끓일 요량으로 냉동실에 얼려놓은 시래기를 꺼낸다. 고향에서 먹던 맛이라며 옥화가 참 잘 먹었던 시래기 된장국이다. "혹시 운이 좋아서 한국까지 살아서 간다면, 이 집

Hong's empty juice cup became thin and transparent. She collapsed it in her hand.

"I won't ever forget that you helped me. Once I make a lot of money later, I'll repay you. And, if I become rich..." the woman stopped. Although Hong repeated that she didn't want to get repaid and that all she wanted was for the woman to be safe, it was of no use. On the contrary, it seemed that asking her to repay was more respectful to her.

The woman traced back the way she had come from the Post Office station. When she got there she took a seat and began to wait for the bus.

"I've never told anyone my stories. I feel better because I told you," the woman said before she got on the bus. She looked more comfortable now.

When the bus left, swaying and lurching a bit, Hong's eyes smarted from the bus' exhaust fumes. "And, if I get rich, I won't be like any of you people." Was this what the woman wanted to say in the end? But, wasn't that something only God would have known, as she'd said? As Hong stared up at the profile of the woman sitting serenely by the window of the bus, she stood alone and coughed.

It was light outside. Hong opened her eyes and

사람들 절대 잊어버리지 않을 거라요. 거기서 벌어서 꼭 갚을 거라요." 떠나가기 전, 옥화는 불쑥 홍에게 엄마가 보고 싶다며 고향에 내려가겠다고 했다. 엄마랑 아무렇지도 않게 평범한 이틀을 같이 보낸 뒤, 그 아이는 언제 있었던 아이냐 싶게 연기처럼 그들의 인생에서 사라진 것이었다. 엄마는 옥화의 편지를, 마을 이장 아저씨한테서 받은, 끝내 실체를 알 수 없는 그녀의 싸인이 적힌 오천 원의 차용증과 같이 홍에게 보여주었다.

그해 늦가을, 옥화가 떠나간 집에 돌아온 남동생은 만취상태에서 오토바이를 타다가 사고를 당했고, 엄마는 아들녀석의 다리가 완쾌되는 것을 보기 전에 뇌출혈로 갑작스레 돌아가셨다. 홍한테는 오천 원의 빚과 엄마를 보낸 슬픔 외에 짝을 잃은 남동생의 허전함을 달래줄 일이 덤으로 남겨진 셈이었다. 그리고 옥화는 여태 아무 소식이 없다. 이날 이때까지.

분주한 아침이 시작되고 있었다. 방문을 벌컥 열어 색색거리며 자는 아들녀석을 소리쳐 깨우고, 씻으라 닦달하고, 밥을 먹여 학교로 보낸다. 집값이 싼 쪽을 택하다 보니 후미진 도시의 변두리로 오게 되는 바람에 녀석의

sat up. Next to her, her husband was sleeping, reeking of booze. It was not clear when he had come home, whether it was past midnight or around dawn. He must have carried materials with the driver yesterday. His hand lay slung across his forehead and she could see a number of new scratches on the back of his hand. He must have been really tired, carrying heavy flooring materials and dealing with the storeowner-customers in anticipation of the collection period. He was the head of their family and responsible for more than ten employees. She looked up at the clock in the living room and quietly tiptoed away. It was Wednesday, October 27, 2013. Hong decided that she should attend the prayer meeting no matter what—for the sake of her son, her husband, their store, and the safety of the woman on her journey.

Hong rushed to wash and cook rice and took out the dried radish leaves from the refrigerator to cook some miso soup. Ok-hwa had loved miso soup with dried radish leaves. She said she'd been used to eating it at home.

Ok-hwa said, "If I am lucky enough to survive on my way to South Korea, I won't forget this family. I'll repay you after I start making money there."

Before Ok-hwa left, she had unexpectedly told

학교까지도 버스로 한 시간 거리다. 창고를 지키는 직원에게서 전화가 온다. 물건이 오는 시간이 앞당겨졌다고, 출근길 차들이 막히기 전에 당장 나와달란다. 말투를 들어보니 고집쟁이 기사 아저씨한테 무슨 불만이 가득 있는 눈치다. 접때처럼 또 어느 직원이 갑자기 그만두는 날엔 큰일이다. 홍은 부리나케 남편을 흔들어 깨우고 부부는 또다시 아침상을 그대로 놓아둔 채 아파트를 나선다.

잠이 덜 깬 남편이 부시시한 얼굴로 차문을 여는 사이, 홍은 두꺼운 장부를 안고 총총걸음으로 1층 리따예네 돼지밭을 지나친다. 어제 금방 옮겨놓은 오이모며 토마토모가 훤칠한 키를 뽐내며 줄느런히 서서 아침햇빛을 받아 마시고 있었다. 그리고 밭 변두리 메마른 땅에서도 작년에 떨어졌을 배추씨 같은 것이 야위고 볼품없으나마 용케 싹을 틔워 자라고 있었다.

홍은 시동을 걸고 있는 남편의 옆자리 조수석에 올라가 앉는다. 햇빛은 언제나처럼 돼지밭 구석구석에 골고루 비추고 있는데, 그 빛을 받은 모종들과 변두리의 싹들이 멀리서 보니 마치 땅에 쓰인 무슨 글씨처럼 보이고 있는 것이었다.

Hong that she missed her mother and wanted to visit her home village. Then after spending two ordinary days with her mother, she had simply vanished. It was as if she'd never been there. Along with Ok-hwa's letter, mother showed Hong a mysterious 5000-*won* I.O.U. with Ok-hwa's signature on it, which the village chief presented to them.

In the late fall that year Hong's brother had returned home to find that Ok-hwa had run away. He had an accident while riding a motorcycle shortly after that. Mother then passed away suddenly from a cerebral hemorrhage before her son's leg fully healed. In addition to 5,000-*won* debt and the pain of losing their mother, Hong also had the burden of comforting her brother, who had suddenly lost his wife. Still, there was no news from Ok-hwa. Not until this very day.

The busy morning routine began. She opened her son's bedroom door without warning, woke him up with a few calls, nagged him into washing himself, and sent him to school.

Since they had had to find a cheaper house, they lived on the outskirts of the city. It took her son an hour to get to his school by bus. She got a call from the warehouse keeper. He told her that the materials would arrive earlier than expected. She should come right away before the morning traffic. His voice suggested that he was very unhappy about their driver and his obstinacy. She and her husband could not afford another sudden employee departure. She woke her husband and they rushed out of their apartment without touching their breakfast.

While her still-sleepy husband was opening their van door, Hong passed by Li Ta-ye's vegetable garden patch on the first floor in a few quick steps, holding the thick accounting book. Young cucumber and tomato plants, transplanted just yesterday, were soaking in the morning sun, standing tall in a row. And on the dry soil near the patch, rows of lettuce, whose seeds must have dropped last year, were pushing out their new, weak sprouts.

Her husband was starting the van and Hong sat on the assistant's seat next to him. The sun was shining across the vegetable garden patches and, seen from afar, the young plants and seedlings looked like marks of writing on the land.

창작노트
Writer's Note

같은 영혼, 다른 역할

가난하다는 이유로 구멍가게 주인아저씨나 식대를 받는 유치원 총무선생님, 그리고 다른 여러 사람들로부터 청하지 않은 도움을 받았던 시절이 있다. 이상하게도 나는 그중 어떤 상황들의 경우, 나를 대하는 그 사람들의 얼굴표정과 목소리의 느낌까지 또렷이 기억하고 있다.

가령, 간장 한 근 값으로 내민 나의 이십 전 중에서 일 전짜리 셋은 밀어 놓으며, "이건 됐다."라고 하시던 가게 주인아저씨의 묘한 웃음 같은 것을 말이다.

원촨 지진(2008년 쓰촨성 대지진) 뒤, 쓰촨에서 올라온 문우를 만난 적이 있다. 일간지의 기자로서 참혹한

Same Soul, Different Roles

There was a time when I received some un-asked-for help from a small neighborhood shop owner, a kindergarten staff member collecting meal payments, and many other people only because they knew that I was poor. I remember in quite vivid detail the smug facial expressions and voices of some of the people at that time who helped me.

I remember the curious smile of the small shop owner who said to me as a child, "That's enough," and pushed back the three pennies out of the twen-ty I had tried to hand him for a gallon of soy sauce.

After the 2008 Wenchuan Great Earthquake I met a writer colleague from Sichuan. She told me that she had been to the disaster zone as a reporter

현장에도 다녀오고 지속적인 후원 사업에도 동참하고 있다는 그녀의 말을 듣고 머리가 뜨거워져, 후원할 만한 아이를 찾아 달라고 부탁했었다. 나는 TV에 나오는 유명 인사들이나 연예인, 거부들처럼 후원금액 숫자가 적힌 커다란 판자를 들고 흔들 생각은 꼬물만치도 없었다.

"내가 내놓을 수 있는 돈은 정말 얼마 안 돼, 그냥 이름 밝히지 않고 그 애가 성인이 될 때까지 쭉 했으면 하는데……." 문우는 거기까지 듣더니, 밥을 먹다 말고 숟가락을 털렁 내려놓는 것이었다. "어쩜 니들은 모두 똑같은 생각을 하는지 모르겠어."하고 그녀는 눈을 동그랗게 뜨고 떨떠름하게 앉아 있는 나를 치켜 보았다. ('니들'이라니? 나만 이런 '고상한' 생각을 하고 있는 줄 알았고만…….)

뭘 잘못한 줄도 모르고 벌을 서는 아이를 취급하는 듯한 그녀의 날카로운 표정과 목소리도, 나는 아마 오랫동안 기억할 것이다. "이름을 밝히지 않으면, 니들은 속이 편할지 모르겠지만 받는 사람이 느끼는 부담감은 생각해봤니? 그들에게 필요한 건 어떤 익명의 사람들이 무상으로 퍼주는 물질적인 도움이 아니라, 정말

and had continued to participate in recovery activities. I was so moved that I asked her to find me a child that I could support. I didn't have any intentions of waving around a large plaque with the donation amount on it, as famous people, celebrities, and millionaires have done on TV.

"I don't really have much money. I just want to continue helping the child until he or she grows up without letting them know who I am—"

Before I could finish my sentence, my colleague put her spoon down loudly in the middle of eating and said, "I wonder how it is that all of you always think the same way." Then, she glared at me while I stared at her wide-eyed, thinking: "All of you?" I thought I was the only one so noble.

I'll also remember her severe expression and voice for a long time, the way she treated me like a child being punished for something she's doesn't even know she's done wrong.

"So, if you help them in secret, I guess that would make all of you feel comfortable. But have you ever thought about the sense of burden that they would feel? What they need isn't material aid showered on them incognito, but human-to-human interest and support."

I remember the furrowed brow of the small shop

로 인격 대 인격적인 관심과 응원이야……."

'쟤는 애비도 없고, 가난하니까…….' 일 전짜리 세
개를 내 손안에 남겨놓고 돌아서서 다른 사람들과 수
군거리던 가게 아저씨의 모여진 눈썹, 그리고 여유 있
는 자들이 지을 수 있는 미소 같은 것이 생각났다. 문
우 앞에 점잖게 앉아 있던 그날의 내 모습이 그 가게
아저씨의 것과 같았단 말인가.

「옥화」를 구상하면서 나는 이 소설이 어떤 체제나 무
슨 주의, 이념 같은 거대담론을 피해서 읽히기를 바랐
다. 경제학자의 이론이 좌판 장사꾼한테는 별로 도움
이 되지 않을 수 있는 것처럼 거시세계와 양자세계에
서 운행되는 법칙은 흔히 다른 법, 나는 미시의 인간
원자들한테 더 관심을 가지는 편이라고 해두고 싶다.

아울러 이 이야기는 사람 사는 곳이면 어디서나 있
을 법한 이야기로서 전혀 새롭거나 낯선 이야기도 아
니다. 지금은 아파트 단지들이 들어서면서 사라졌지
만 불과 칠팔 년 전까지 전형적인 조선족 동네의 모습
을 하고 있던 고향마을에는 1990년대 초반 전후로 수
십 명의 '북조선' 여자와 남자들이 거쳐 갔다. 중국이란
다민족 국가에서 극적으로 만난 이들과의 조우는 아

owner who'd whispered to the others at the store after leaving the three pennies in my palm, "She doesn't have a father and she's poor, you know." I can also remember the complacent smiles of those who had more than enough. Was the polite attitude I'd struck in front of my writer colleague the same as that of the shop owner?

When I was writing "Ok-hwa," I hoped that it would be read outside the context of some grand discourse on systemic failures or ideology. Economic theory isn't much help to pushcart peddlers. The laws of the world as a whole and the laws of the quantum world are quite different from each other. I just would like to say I'm more interested in the world from a micro-human quantum level.

Also, what "Ok-hwa" deals with is not new or strange, but something that can happen anywhere. My hometown used to look like a typical traditional Korean village until seven or eight years ago, when it changed with the arrival of the boom in apartment complexes. Scores of North Korean women and men passed through that village around the early 1990s. During this dramatic encounter between Koreans from a multi-ethnic China and North Koreans, my hometown residents, who retained a "blood consciousness" mentality, were in-

직 '핏줄의식'을 놓지 않고 있던 고향 사람들에게 본능적인 이끌림과 더불어 그들의 처지에 대한 측은함을 유발시킨 것은 당연한 일이다.

그렇게 시작된 그들과의 인연, 짧게는 반년에서 일년, 길게는 칠팔 년까지 그들과 가족관계를 영위해온 이들도 있다. 그리고 그동안 인류역사가 시작되면서부터 내내 되풀이되던 이야기들이 생긴 것이다.

고향사람들한테 그 이야기들이 별로 낯설지 않게 느껴지던 것은, 또 다른 구체적인 우연성 때문이었을 거다. 입장이 다소 바뀌긴 했지만 1992년 한중 수교 이후 다시 이어지게 된 '남조선' 사람들과의 만남에서 비롯된 여러 이야기들이 말이다.

때는 이미 '흑묘백묘' 연설이 있고 난 뒤였다. '집체호'시절을 온전히 겪고 나서도 한동안 '집체의식 평등분배'를 껴안고 방황하다가, 그즈음에야 비로소 '세 개의 사과를 두 사람이 나누는 문제'(평등분배 원칙을 깨뜨린 문제로, 유독 중국 아이들에게 난제였다는 수학문제)에 대해 곤혹스러움을 느끼지 않을 수 있었던 시절이었다.

그러니 삼 전을 깎아준 가게 아저씨한테 예의상 머

stinctively attracted to those poor North Koreans and pitied them. It was all very natural.

These relationships that began in this way lasted from half a year to a year. Some families even lasted seven or eight years. At the same time, as has happened from time immemorial, stories of distrust, prejudice, and complacency arose.

To the people in my hometown, these negative stories didn't feel that odd because of another relationship. There were many similar stories from their encounters with South Koreans—but this time with the power dynamic reversed. These stories had been told since the 1992 establishment of South Korea and China's official relationship. It was after Dèng Xioping's famous Black Cat/White Cat address. We had already left behind the time of collectivism, no longer worrying about "collective-style equal distribution." Children no longer had the challenge of solving the problem of how to divide three apples between two people.

No wonder my childhood self, who'd felt hurt even while bowing to thank the shop owner who had just returned my three pennies, had become an adult who could complacently smile and say, "I just want to help in secret." After experiencing both communism and private ownership, poverty and

리 숙여 인사를 하면서도 마음이 내내 불편했던 어린 시절의 내가, 어느새 '이름 밝히지 않고 그냥 도와줬으면 한다.'고 여유 있게 미소 지을 수 있는 어른이 되어 버린 것이었다. 공유와 사유, 가난과 풍요, 받는 자와 주는 자……. 이쪽과 저쪽의 역할을 대강 겪어보고 나니 「옥화」를 쓰고 싶다는 생각이 들었다.

섣부른 동정이 때론 비난보다 못할 수가 있듯이, 이 이야기에 대해서도 어떤 섣부른 결말을 내릴 생각은 없다. 우리는 모두 삶이라는 과정을 거쳐 가고 있는 인간일 뿐이니까. 또한, 우리 모두에게 있어서 시초에 똑같은 영혼이 주어졌다는 것을 상기하고 나면 후천적으로 보태지는 약간의 빛깔과 껍질에 대해 도무지 동정이나 비난 같은 것을 할 수가 없게 되는 법이기도 하다.

어떠한 경우에도 '은혜'란, 사람이 사람한테 베푸는 것이 아니며, 진정한 '선행'은 자신의 행위를 인식하지 못할 때 가능한 것이며, 사람이 사람한테 줄 수 있는 것, 그리고 마땅히 주어야 하는 것은 '존중'뿐임을 새삼 깨닫는다.

그런데 그렇게 생각하면서 주위를 둘러보니, 이미 그리 살다간 선인들이며, 지금 그리 살고 있는 소박한 사

wealth, receiving and giving, I felt I could finally write "Ok-hwa."

Since clumsy pity can sometimes be worse than judgment, I don't want to present any haphazard conclusions to this story. We're all human beings who have to go through this thing called life. And if we remember that we've all been given the same soul, we can't pity or criticize someone for the little bit of tan color or skin added to it later.

Whatever the circumstances, a blessing isn't something one human being can give to another. A true good deed is possible only when we're not aware of it. The only thing a human being can, and must, give another human being is respect. These are things I realize anew.

When I look around with this thought in mind, I can see many simple predecessors and contemporaries who have practiced this way of thinking all over the world. And I now no longer feel that lonely.

From Changchun
April 2014

람들이 지구촌 구석구석 띄엄띄엄 보이고 있어서 너무
외롭지는 않았다.

2014년 4월 창춘에서

해설
Commentary

탈북자를 바라보는 또 하나의 눈

이경재 (문학평론가)

현재 탈북자 숫자는 이만오천여 명에 이르고 있다. 이
것은 1990년대 중후반 이후에 탈북자의 정체성이 변모
하며, 그 숫자가 대량으로 증가한 결과이다. 1990년대
중반 이전까지의 탈북이 소수에게 국한된, 정치적 성격
을 지닌 것이었다면, 이후의 탈북은 생존을 목적으로
한 경제적 성격을 지니게 되었다. 어떠한 방식으로든
현실과 관련을 맺을 수밖에 없는 소설 장르의 특성상,
2000년대 한국 소설에서 탈북자들을 다룬 경우는 어렵
지 않게 발견할 수 있다. 금희의「옥화」는 조선족 사회
의 탈북자라는 매우 독특한 소재를 다루고 있다. 이것
은 작가인 금희가 1979년 중국 지린성 주타이시에서

Another Perspective on North Korean Escapees

Lee Kyung-jae (literary critic)

As of April 2014, the total number of North Korean escapees amounts to around 25,000. The dramatic increase in their numbers since the 1990s is most likely due to changes in the nature and motivation of these escapees. While a small minority of North Koreans left their country for political reasons before then, a much larger number have been escaping since then for economic reasons—that is, for basic survival needs.

Since short stories and novels tend to deal with reality in whatever way the time and place presents it, we now have a multitude of fictional works that deal with the realities of North Korean escapees. "Ok-hwa" by Geum-Hee is a particularly unusual

출생한 조선족이라는 사실과 밀접하게 연관된 것으로
보인다.

1945년부터 1999년까지의 조선족 문학은 크게 정치
공명시기(1945년~1978년)와 다원화시기(1979년~1999
년)로 나뉜다. 개혁 개방을 기점으로 하여 극단적인 정
치화와 공리주의 가치관을 획일적으로 드러내던 모습
에서 벗어나 다양한 주제와 다원적인 가치관을 추구하
는 방향으로 변한 것이다. 이러한 변화는 "국가언어에
서 개인언어로의 변화"[1]라고 정리해 볼 수 있다. 금희의
「옥화」 역시도 조선족 문학이 거쳐 온 큰 변화의 연장선
상에 놓인 작품으로서, 탈북자라는 사회적 문제를 이념
과 같은 거대담론이 아닌 한 개인의 내면 심리를 통해
섬세하게 추적하고 있다.

최근의 한국소설이 탈북자를 다루는 시각은 세 가지
정도로 나누어 볼 수 있다. 그 중의 대표적인 것은 탈북
자를 남한 자본주의 사회의 비정함을 비판하기 위한 대
상으로 바라보는 것이다. 다음으로 탈북자를 통해 북한
체제의 문제를 직접적으로 드러내는 경우도 있다. 마지

1) 김동훈·최삼룡·오상순·장춘식, 『중국조선족문학사』, 민족출판사, 2007,
339면.

portrayal of North Korean refugees living in ethnically Korean communities in China. Among the many reasons for taking this angle on the genre depicting North Korean escapees, it's likely that her upbringing has a great to deal to do with it, since the author is a Korean-Chinese native of Jiutai City in the Jilin Province of China.

Korean literature by ethnically Korean writers in China from 1945 to 1999 can usually be divided into two periods: political fellowship (1945-78) and polycentrism (1979-99). Generally, this shift can be characterized as moving from extreme politicization and utilitarianism to the acceptance of different themes and perspectives after China's reform. One might dub this as a change from national language to individual language. Geum Hee's "Ok-hwa" reflects this change since it approaches the social problem of North Korean escapees not from a macro level, or an ideological point of view, but through an individual's interior psychology.

The way that Korean novels and stories have recently dealt with North Korean escapees can be divided into three categories. One criticizes the heartlessness of South Korean capitalist society through the experiences of North Korean escapees, another directly exposes the North Korean re-

막으로는 전지구적으로 나타나고 있는 디아스포라 현상의 대표적인 사례로 탈북자를 다루는 경우이다. 금희의「옥화」는 마지막 경향에 해당하는 작품으로서, 이 작품에 등장하는 탈북자인 옥화와 여자는 조선족 마을을 거쳐 한국 등으로 떠나간다.

이 작품의 초점화자는 조선족인 홍이다. 조선족의 눈에 비친 탈북자는 배은망덕한 존재들이다. 조선족들의 눈에 탈북한 '여자'는 꾀병을 부리고 일자리를 구해주어 봤자 갖가지 핑계를 대며 일을 하지 않는 사람이다. 나아가 그 여자는 "인간으로서 기본적인 도덕이나 정직한 양심 따위마저 있는지 여부가 의심스러운 사람"으로까지 인식 된다. 여자는 한때 홍의 올케였던 옥화와 뒤태는 물론이고 분위기까지 비슷하다. 옥화의 경우에는 동생과 가족을 버리고 도망가버려, 홍의 가족을 거의 파탄에 이르게 만들었다.

탈북자인 옥화와 여자는 조선족 사람들이 베푼 호의를 고까워하며 은혜를 갚기는커녕 도망치듯 다른 곳으로 떠나간다. 여자가 돈을 꿔달라고 한 이후 홍이 꾸는 꿈속에서, 여자는 홍의 도움에 감사하기는커녕 "그 잘난 돈, 개도 안 먹는 돈, 그딴 거 쪼꼼 던재준 거 내 하나

gime, and the third comprises stories that deal with North Korean escapees as examples of global diaspora. The short story "Ok-hwa," with the protagonist and an unnamed woman migrating from North Korea, through the ethnic Korean villages in China, and finally to South Korea, belongs in this last category.

"Ok-hwa" is written primarily from the perspective of Hong, an ethnic Korean in China. To such people, North Korean escapees are all ingrates. The unnamed female North Korean escapee initially seems to fit the mold. She appears to feign poor health and come up with every possible excuse not to work at jobs that people find for her. At one point, she is even perceived as a "person with questionable moral beliefs, someone who did not seem to possess an honest conscience." She has a "particular North Korean scent" and "the sort of aura that reminded her [Hong] of Ok-hwa," Hong's sister-in-law and an eventual, highly unfortunate escapee as well.

An additional unexpected link between Ok-hwa and the woman is that not only do they both leave without warning, but both also seem highly ungrateful to the ethnic Koreans who offer them help along the way. Instead of repaying their hosts' gen-

도 안 고맙다요."라며 비난한다. 그리고 "한국 가서 돈 많이 벌어바라, 내는 너들처럼 안 기래"라며 더욱 홍을 불편하게 한다. 김치쪼가리와 밥덩어리도 주었지만, 탈북자들은 감사해 하지도 않으며 고까워하기나 하는 것이다. 이러한 탈북자들의 모습이야말로 바로 홍(조선족)이 겪는 심리적 불편함의 핵심이다.

그러나 홍과 여자가 나누는 대화를 통해 조선족들이 지닌 탈북자들에 대한 인식은 조선족들의 선입견에 불과하다는 사실이 드러난다. "한 사람이 어떻다는 거이는 하느님만 아시디, 딴 사람들은 다 모른다는 거이요."라는 말처럼, 조선족들은 탈북자 일반에 대한 선입견으로 여자를 대했을 뿐, 고유한 개인으로서의 탈북자에는 아무런 관심도 없다. 조선족들은 여자가 북한을 탈출하여 사람 장사꾼한테 잡혀서 허베이성 산골 오지에 팔렸다가, 애까지 낳은 후에 혼자 도망쳐 나온 과거 따위는 전혀 모르는 것이다. 그런데도 교회 사람들은 여자를 중간에 앉혀 놓고 죄인 심판하듯이 질책의 말을 쏟아놓는다. 여자의 말을 들으며 홍은 "부유하고, 학식있고, 덕망있고……. 또 '믿음' 있는 사람들에게 둘러싸여 죄인이 된 그날의 여자"를 눈앞에 떠올린다. 그제야 비로소

erosity, they leave as if fleeing from them. At one point, Hong has a dream, after being asked to lend the woman more money, in which the woman criticizes Hong: "Oh, all that money! Money even a dog couldn't use! So you throw a little bit of money at me. No, I'm not grateful! Who do you think you are?" Later on, she makes Hong even more uncomfortable: "Once I make a lot of money in South Korea, then I won't behave like you guys." Although people give her *kimchi* and several portions of rice, the two North Korean escapees seem more spiteful than grateful. It is this attitude that is the essence of what makes Hong and other ethnic Koreans in China psychologically uncomfortable.

However, during a later conversation between Hong and the woman, Hong's understanding of North Korean escapees proves to be more a matter of prejudice than anything else. As the escapee points out: "it is only God and no one else that can understand a person." The Koreans in China view North Korean escapees through their prejudices rather than as unique individuals. They don't know or care that this particular woman escaped North Korea, was sold through human traffickers to a family in a remote mountain area, and eventually ran away after giving birth. Still, these Christians

조선족들로부터 여자가 받은 것들이 "'그 잘란 것, 그딴 거'따위"가 된 이유를 어렴풋하게 이해한다. 그러고 보면 엄마가 옥화를 처음 데려왔을 때 엄마가 냈던 "백화점 세일을 만나 명품을 헐값으로 사온 듯한 흥분된 목소리" 속에도 사물화 된 옥화의 모습이 분명하게 아로새겨져 있다.

조선족들은 탈북자들을 단독성을 지닌 고유한 인간이 아니라, 김치쪼가리나 밥덩어리에 감지덕지할 불쌍한 자라는 특수한 위치에 자리매김하고서는 그 틀만으로 그들을 바라보았던 것이다. 그 결과 여자는 "사람들은 여기서 일도 하고 맘에 맞는 사람 만나 살라디만, 긴데 기실 여기서는 하고 싶은 거 아무거이두 못해요. 거기 가므는 합법적으루 뭐이나 할 수 있대니, 가야디요." 라고 말한다.

홍이 여자를 이해하는 데에는 한국에서 삼사 년간 일하고 돌아온 시형의 존재도 큰 역할을 한다. 시형의 겉모습은 거짓말처럼 땟물을 쏙 벗고 허여멀쑥하니 변해 있었지만, "힘든 노동, 사람들의 배척과 편견, 보장받지 못하는 인권"으로 인하여 "그곳에서의 정착은 아직 미래가 명랑하지 못하"다고 말한다. 시형은 술에 취해서

practically interrogated her like a criminal. Listening to this story, Hong can "see the woman as a criminal surrounded by those who were wealthy, intelligent, and virtuous...believers." It is finally here when Hong vaguely understands why she says of fellow Christians' help: "Oh, all that money! Money even a dog couldn't use!" Additionally, Hong remembers her own mother's excited voice when she brought Ok-hwa home, how her tone was like that of a woman who "had just had bought luxury merchandise at bargain prices at a department store sale." Ok-hwa was reified rather than humanized.

Geum Hee's story seems to make the point that ethnic Koreans'perspectives of North Koreans define the latter not as unique and equal human beings but as supplicants who should be grateful for even a few meager offerings of *kimchi* and rice. The woman notes this as well: "People told me to marry and just look for any kind of job here, but I can do nothing I want here. Since I heard that I could do anything legally there [South Korea], I have to go."

Hong can understand the woman better thanks to her brother-in-law's visit after he returns from a few years of migrant work in South Korea. His appearance has changed and he looks less tanned

는 "에이, 못사는 게 죄지. 잘사는 나라에 살지 않는다고 대우가 이렇게 다르니"라고까지 말하는 것이다. 옥화는 시형네도 "여자처럼? 옥화처럼?" 생활한 것인가라는 질문을 갖게 된다. 시형네는 아무도 알지 못하고 아무도 믿을 수 없는 상황에서 누구에게도 진실한 이야기를 할 수 없었다고 말한다. "자기편이 아닌 땅에서 살아가는 이들의 불안함"은 그들을 더욱 폐쇄적이고 불투명한 존재로 만들었던 것이다. 그리고 보면 옥화를 비롯한 북녘 여자들 누구도 "가야 하는 이유를 아무한테도 말"하지 않은 채 떠나갔다. 홍의 시형네를 통해 알 수 있듯이, 조선족과 탈북자 사이에서 벌어지는 비윤리적 인간관계는 한국인과 조선족 사이에서 그대로 벌어지고 있었던 것이다. 그렇다면 한국행을 선택한 옥화나 여자의 미래도 결코 밝지만은 않을 것이 분명하다.

「옥화」는 탈북자와 관련해 한국소설에 빈 칸으로 남아 있던 많은 부분을 채워주고 있다. 한국소설에서 탈북자와 조선족은 이주노동자나 결혼이민자로서 한국사회의 타자라는 같은 범주로 묶여서 이해되고는 하였다. 특히 이들은 한민족이라는 한 덩어리로서 이해되었고 그들 사이의 차이는 거의 고려되지 않았다. 그러나

and much paler. He says: "The prospect of future settlements was not quite bright yet," attributing this to "hard labor, exclusion and prejudice, human rights violations, and so on." After getting drunk, he adds: "Huh, to be poor is to be guilty. Look how differently they treat you just because you're from a poor country!"

Hong wonders if her brother- and sister-in-law are living in South Korea in a manner similar to the Korean escapee in China. She ponders if they are living "like the woman? Or perhaps even Ok-hwa?" Hong's brother-in-law says that he and his wife cannot trust and tell their true stories to anyone. "The anxiety of all those who lived in the land of people not on their side" turns them into people less open and more opaque. Ok-hwa, along with other North Korean women, left without "clarify[ing] why she had to go." Thus, the same unethical human relationship between ethnic Koreans in China and North Korean escapees repeats itself between South Koreans and ethnic Korean Chinese migrant workers. From this, it is also clear that the futures of Ok-hwa and the woman who eventually ends up in South Korea likely aren't very bright.

"Ok-hwa" fleshes out the Korean understanding of North Korean escapees. In most Korean litera-

조선족 작가 금희를 통하여 이들 사이의 공통점과 차이점이 섬세하게 구분되고 있다. 고유성이 전혀 고려되지 않는 것이야말로 타자화의 가장 큰 문제라는 사실에 비춰볼 때, 조선족과 탈북자가 지닌 고유성에 대한 인식은 올바른 인식을 위한 중요한 계기가 될 수 있다. 나아가 이 작품은 진정으로 남을 돕는다는 것이 무엇인지를, 인간을 떠돌이로 만드는 '불안'이 무엇인지를 고민하게끔 만드는 작품이기도 하다.

ture, North Korean escapees and ethnic Korean Chinese migrant workers are understood as the ethnic "other" of Korean society, as just migrant workers and marital-citizenship immigrants. In particular, North Korean escapees and ethnic Korean Chinese migrant workers have often been lumped together as having the same ethnic origins irrespective of their differences. "Ok-hwa" reveals these differences, as well as their commonalities. Disrespect for a person's singularity is the greatest problem of "otherization," but this story's careful examination of the differences between North Korean escapees and ethnic Koreans in China can provide a solid foundation for our deepened understanding of their individuality. Ultimately, "Ok-hwa" urges us to think deeply about what it means to help others, and what would make others so "anxious" that they would have to flee.

비평의 목소리
Critical Acclaim

금희 작품에서 또 하나 우리가 유의해야 할 것은 이
야기 꾸밈능력과 언어사용이다. 금희는 자기의 생활체
험을 형상화하기 위해 늘 자신의 주변에서 일어나거나,
자신이 일찍 경험했거나 보아왔던 평범한 일상으로 소
설을 꾸미고 있는데 그런 잡다한 이야기들을 소설화하
면서도 그러한 것들을 아무런 여과 없이 소설에 도입하
는 것이 아니라 그 가운데서 자신의 생활체험을 가장
집약적으로 반영할 수 있는 부분들을 선택하여 소설에
기입한다. 이러한 기입을 위해 작가는 또 우연한 만남
이란 소설적 장치를 사용하기도 하는데 위에서 언급한
「뻐스정류장에 핀 아이리스」에서 나오는 상과의 만남,

Geum Hee's fiction is noteworthy for both her ability to construct a story and her use of language. She often uses ordinary, everyday details from her experiences and observations. She doesn't randomly choose miscellaneous details, however, but only those that succinctly convey the essence of an experience. Often she uses the fictional device of a chance meeting to effectively organize the details. The characters Shang in "Irises at the Bus Stop" and Uncle and Brother in "Swallow, Swallow" are introduced into this fictional device, adding interest while serving the purpose of the story. Furthermore, the beginnings and the endings of her stories are neatly dovetailed, involving Shang in "Irises

그리고 소설 결말 부분의 샹,「제비야 제비야」에 나오는 삼촌과 오빠의 어제와 오늘 등등은 모두 이러한 소설적 장치로서 어찌 보면 우연인 것 같지만 소설의 슈제트를 꾸밈에 있어서 모두 필요하고도 자연스럽게 쓰이면서 소설에 재미를 더해주고 있으며「뻐스정류장에 핀 아이리스」에 등장하는 샹,「제비야 제비야」에서의 제비,「파란 리봉의 모자를 쓴 소녀」중의 그림 등등도 모두와 결말 부분이 묘한 조응관계를 이루며 기다란 여운을 남기고 있다. 특히「뻐스정류장에 핀 아이리스」에 등장하는 샹은 결말 부분에서 명확한 해답을 주지 않고 그 답을 독자들에게 남김으로써 깊이 있는 여운을 길게 만들고 있는데 이러한 것들은 모두 작가의 소설 꾸밈방식에 대한 부단한 탐구와 직결되어 있는 것이라고 하겠다.

이진윤, 「금희 소설의 예술적 특징」,

『슈뢰딩거의 상자』, 료녕민족출판사, 2013

at the Bus Stop,"the swallow in "Swallow, Swallow," and a picture in "A Girl Wearing a Hat with a Blue Ribbon." This clever agreement generates far-reaching resonances; in particular, in "Irises at the Bus Stop," Shang does not offer a clear resolution, but instead leaves the task in the hands of the reader, thus offering us opportunities to reflect deeply on it. All these devices clearly reveal the author's persistent exploration into the methods of fictional construction.

Yi Jin-yun, "Artistic Characteristics of Geum Hee's Fiction,"

Schrödinger's Box (Liaoning Nationality Publishing House, 2013)

K-픽션 009
옥화

2015년 8월 3일 초판 1쇄 발행

지은이 금희 | 옮긴이 전승희 | 펴낸이 김재범
기획위원 정은경, 전성태, 이경재
편집 정수인, 윤단비, 김형욱 | 관리 박신영
펴낸곳 (주)아시아 | 출판등록 2006년 1월 27일 제406-2006-000004호
주소 서울특별시 동작구 서달로 161-1(흑석동 100-16)
전화 02.821.5055 | 팩스 02.821.5057 | 홈페이지 www.bookasia.org
ISBN 979-11-5662-123-2(set) | 979-11-5662-124-9 (04810)
값은 뒤표지에 있습니다.

K-Fiction 009
Ok-hwa

Written by Geum Hee | **Translated by** Jeon Seung-hee
Published by ASIA Publishers | 161-1, Seodal-ro, Dongjak-gu, Seoul, Korea
Homepage Address www.bookasia.org | **Tel**. (822).821.5055 | **Fax**. (822).821.5057
First published in Korea by ASIA Publishers 2015
ISBN 979-11-5662-123-2(set) | 979-11-5662-124-9 (04810)

한국문학의 가장 중요하고 첨예한 문제의식을 가진 작가들의 대표작을 주제별로 선정!
하버드 한국학 연구원 및 세계 각국의 한국문학 전문 번역진이 참여한 번역 시리즈!
미국 하버드대학교와 컬럼비아대학교 동아시아학과, 캐나다 브리티시컬럼비아대학교 아시아
학과 등 해외 대학에서 교재로 채택!

바이링궐 에디션 한국 대표 소설 set 3

금기와 욕망 Taboo and Desire

바이링궐 에디션 한국 대표 소설 set 6

운명 Fate

미의 사제들 Aesthetic Priests

식민지의 벌거벗은 자들 The Naked in the Colony

바이링궐 에디션 한국 대표 소설 set 7

백치가 된 식민지 지식인 Colonial Intellectuals Turned "Idiots"